A

Gulf Coast Paranormal

Season Two Book Three

By M.L. Bullock and Kevin Bullock

Dedication

To all who are lost.

Chapter One—Midas

It had been months since the last time I investigated the paranormal with my team. My team. Were they still my team?

So much had taken place since that time—would they still have faith in me? Sierra had been taking the lead these past months and doing a good job of everything. I never had any doubts she would. But it was time. I was feeling the itch. I missed them, missed what we do.

Would the team still believe in me? I had so many unanswered questions. Did they blame me for Jocelyn's death since I was leading them? They said they didn't, but who knows?

Was I ready to get back in the thick of things? *Ready or not, here I come.*

Why was this case pulling me in? What was in that cave? I was full of questions and concerns. The only way I was going to get answers was to engage with the team and pick up my calling.

Wait a minute...I am a dad now with a beautiful baby boy and a wonderful wife wanting to spend her life with me. Are dads supposed to do these kinds of things?

Should I quit and take care of Cassidy and our son? Cassidy would not want me to quit; she knows how much I want to help people. It's settled, then.

I am going to do this—I am going to do what fulfills me and brings me joy. I just need to take precautions to ensure that the team is safe and I can come back home to my family whole. And so can the team.

I picked up the phone and tapped on a familiar number. "Hello? Sierra?" May as well jump right in. "This is Midas. Would you like to go with me to Goliath Cave?"

There was a long silence on the line. "Sure, Midas, but why do you need me?" Sierra asked cautiously.

I cleared my throat nervously. "Well, you have been leading the team in my absence, and I wanted to include you. I wouldn't want to do this without you."

With relief in her voice, Sierra practically squealed, "That sounds great! When would you like to go?"

I shared a few details and let her know this was an urgent case.

"Butch is an experienced climber. I think he'd be a big help. God knows I can't climb at all. Should I put a call in to him?"

"Yes, contact him for me so he can be prepared. I will get back to you as soon as I get the appointment scheduled with the caretaker. Give me a few days, and I will call you back."

"Great, Midas. It is so good to hear from you, and I'm looking forward to having you lead the team again. We sure have missed you! I never understood the pressure you were under before, but I do now. Please take this job back," Sierra said seriously.

"I'm back."

"Talk to you soon, then. I'll tell Joshua. He's going to lose his mind! Bye, and give my love to Cassidy and Dominic."

"Will do." I smiled as I hung up the phone. Wow, that went better than I expected. I guess I overthought that. I decided to make the call.

"Hello, Mr. Jonas? This is Midas from Gulf Coast Paranormal. I received your email about the unusual things happening in Goliath Cave. I just spoke with my team. We're interested in helping you."

"Yes, Midas, it is good to hear from you. How is your family doing?" Although his voice was smooth, I could hear the age and concern in his tone.

"They are doing very well. Thank you for asking. Tell me about what is happening in the caves."

"Where to begin? But I have a question. Please don't think me rude for asking. How are you coping with the death of one of your team members? I know that pain, I am afraid."

It was surprising that Jonas would know this about me. I guess it was no secret. "We will always miss Jocelyn. All we can do is carry on." I stiffened at this strange question-and-answer session.

"I know the type of pressure leadership brings. It can cause doubts and fears. But I sense that you are a strong man with a solid foundation."

I shook my head, unsure what to say. "Um, thanks. About the activity..."

"You may or may not know that these caves have a history of people disappearing in them. Back in the '50s or '60s, there was talk of gemstones in the caves, which brought out the treasure seekers. We hear voices and knocking sounds. There has been at least one report of a black shadowy figure in the deepest part of the cave.

It's not an ordinary shadow. It moves in a way that isn't normal. All I can say is that it is not normal," Jonas replied worriedly.

"Sounds like a lot is going on in the cave. Has anyone been touched or hurt?"

"No, no one has had any physical encounters. Yet. But I can't help but feel that it is possible, and this is a dangerous environment. Lots of places to fall and disappear. Mostly in and around the largest cave, Goliath. It is truly a monster of a cave."

"Glad to hear no one has been hurt. When can I bring the team to check it out? We can be there in 48 hours."

"That sounds great, Midas. Great. I will be expecting you and your team. Just meet me at the caretaker's house, and I will show you around."

"Great, Mr. Jonas, looking forward to meeting you in person also. Goodbye, sir."

He hung up the phone, and I was left staring at mine. How did he know about my family, and how did he know about the death of Jocelyn? Maybe he saw it on social media. That was a bit strange, though. *Okay, I'm not going to freak out about it. I have a job to do.* May as well make it official.

"Wow, that was fast, Big Brother."

"Yep, pretty fast. It's a go. Have the team meet me at the office tomorrow at 8 a.m. They should be packed and ready to go to Woodville, Alabama. We are scheduled to meet the caretaker of Goliath Cave, Mr. Jonas, within 48 hours. It is a serious case, and they need our help."

"Sure thing, Midas. I will contact them right now. Is Cassidy coming too? How's she doing?"

"She's great, Sierra. Feeling better every day. I don't think she'll go on this trip with us, but she will no doubt be painting. I am looking forward to seeing everyone. And Macie... Is she ready mentally and emotionally?"

"She is as right as rain, Big Brother. No need to worry. Jericho will be with her, and we'll keep her close. Promise. The team will see you tomorrow. Bye. Emily is having a hissy fit about something or other. I'd better rescue the dog."

I laughed at hearing about her daughter's antics. That was one spirited child. Just like her mother. "Goodbye, Sierra, and good luck!"

I heard the front door open. Cassidy came inside with Dominic in his carrier and bags dangling off her arm. She'd gotten up early to go do some grocery shopping. I loved my beautiful wife.

She'd braided her long red hair, and the braid was cascading over her shoulder. She still had a great tan from our time in Greece. I was a lucky guy.

"Midas? Where are you?"

"Here, baby. Let me have Dominic. Wow, did you leave anything in the produce section?"

She laughed and kissed me as I took Dominic. He was fast asleep. I set him carefully on the floor near the bar.

"I just hung up with Little Sister. She asked about you. I asked her to get the team ready for Goliath Cave."

She smiled her beautiful smile as she unpacked the grocery bags. "I bet they are stoked that you're back."

I grinned but shook my head. I wasn't sure. Not until I saw their faces. "We will see tomorrow at 8 a.m. That is when we will leave for Goliath Cave. Will you and the baby be okay in the hotel room? Or would you rather stay home? It's up to you, baby."

"Wild horses couldn't keep me away. From you or the team. Of course we will be okay, Midas. Let's get the hotel rooms booked and start packing. Everything will be fine! Dominic is a regular world traveler at this point."

She slid into my arms, and I couldn't resist stealing another kiss. "Okay, let's not forget how we ended up with the last bundle of joy. Easy, tiger." Cassidy said playfully.

"Cassidy, I love you!"

"I love you too, Midas. Now, let's get busy."

*****

"Good morning, everyone. I am glad you could be here on such short notice. I appreciate you. We have a serious case, and the client is desperate for our help."

"Wait! Before you get started, come on out, Cassidy."

To my surprise, my wife walked out of the supply room with a cake. Chocolate, of course. My favorite. There was a single candle burning. Someone had taken the time to frost the words "Welcome back, Midas" on the top. I couldn't hide the tears in my eyes.

Man, I wasn't expecting to cry today. These crazies are truly my family.

In between bites of cake, everyone welcomed me back with words of support and hugs. I barely had a chance to tell them what was happening on the case. Eventually, we all settled back into our chairs. Wow, the Gulf Coast Paranormal office was full again. This was a great feeling.

"Okay, back to the details. Thank you for the cake, guys. God knows I am so grateful to be back. I couldn't do this without you. Nor would I want to. Macie, Joshua, Sierra, Butch, and Jericho—Thank you. Each of you." Sherman groaned at Macie's feet. "Sorry. You too, Sherman."

"Enough with the sappy stuff. Give us the deets, boss," Joshua said as he put his plate down.

"Alright. The caretaker's name is Leeland Jonas, an elderly gentleman who is very knowledgeable about the caves. I couldn't guess how long he's been there. The guests and his fellow volunteers have reported voices in areas where there should be no voices. Knocking sounds, too."

"Tommyknockers?" Jericho asked.

His question made my skin crawl. "Maybe. I don't know. There is at least one report of a shadow figure. No one has had any physical encounters with anything, but a teenager went missing in the caves several years ago. He was never found. We can't let our guard down, and we should expect anything."

Butch whistled at that news, and the room went quiet. "Yeah, I remember that. I knew the kid."

I cleared my throat. "Cassidy and the baby will stay in the hotel room, and she will keep us updated on any images she paints. Joshua, be prepared for a wet environment and low signal strength. We will be underground most of the time."

"Got you covered."

"Everyone, please be prepared for rough terrain and cool temperatures inside the caves. Butch, we will be depending on your expertise here. I admit I don't know much about caving, but I hear you are a pro."

"I have a healthy respect for those caves. That's for sure. I've got plenty of equipment and some emergency air tanks, in case we need them."

"Sounds like we're ready to roll, then. Let's load up and get going."

Everyone began chattering at once. Joshua and Butch lugged out the heavy gear. We would take the Gulf Coast Paranormal van and my SUV. Little Sister brushed away a tear and turned away.

"No crying, Little Sister. You have been on top of everything. Thank you for letting me work all this out in my head."

"Just trying to do my part and keep our dream alive, Midas. I knew you would be back. You can't help yourself." I hugged her and messed up her hair.

She complained good-naturedly, "Okay, cut it out, jerk. Time to get moving. But I'm going to stop in the ladies' room first. We have about a six-hour drive ahead of us. I hate public restrooms, and I don't think I can hold it for longer than six hours."

"Well, there's always the side of the road," I joked with her.

"I'm never doing that again. You knew Joshua was going to kick the high beams on me, didn't you?"

I laughed and denied everything.

Just like old times.

Chapter Two—Midas

The long drive did a number on my back, but it was nothing compared to the twelve-hour flight from Greece. Still, I didn't regret it. Leaving the team, yes, I regretted that. But I needed time to clear my head—and my soul. Seeing the extended family did me a world of good. They embraced Cassidy with open arms, as if they'd always known her. The Demopolis clan was like that. They never met a stranger. There was a language barrier, of course, but love had no barriers. Spending time near the water, holding Cassidy's hand, and kissing her had done so much for me.

But after some time, I was glad to be back on the Gulf Coast. Strange how this haunted and somewhat mysterious place felt like home now. I slept like a log. Thankfully, my son slept through the night too, giving his mother a well-needed break. I didn't expect to be up so early, but my phone buzzed nonstop.

I rubbed my eyes and reached for it as I stumbled toward the curtained window. No need to turn on any lights. I might wake up the baby. Peeling back the curtain a tad, I stared down at the screen. It was still dark out. What time was it? According to my watch, it was barely five in the morning.

Mr. Jonas was calling. Hurrying off to the restroom, I answered, "Mr. Jonas? Is everything okay, sir?"

"I need to meet you at the cave entrance. Now, please. There's not much time." The old man's voice wavered a bit; he sounded weak and sad. This was not the energetic man I'd spoken to the other day.

"Um, okay. I can be there in twenty minutes."

"Thank you. I'll see you at the cave entrance. Please don't be late."

"No problem," I answered, but he'd already hung up. What was going on? Should I wake up Joshua or Sierra? This was certainly unusual, but I wasn't afraid to meet Mr. Jonas. He was a harmless elderly man with real concerns about the caves. Still, it was a strange request. I quietly and hurriedly got dressed. To my surprise, neither my wife nor my son stirred. But I would never leave without kissing her goodbye. It was a promise we made to one another a long time ago.

I pushed back a strand of her red hair and kissed her cheek. She stirred, and her eyes flickered open. Even in the darkness, they were lovely. Just like Cassidy. "I have to go. Mr. Jonas wants to meet me."

"Why? What time is it?"

"It's early. Go back to sleep, Cassidy. I'll be back in time for breakfast."

Despite my attempt to play it cool, she sat up in the bed and took my hands. "Are you sure this is a good idea? Let us go with you," she pleaded in a sleepy voice.

"Don't wake him up. I'll be fine. I'm going to meet Mr. Jonas for a few minutes, then I'll be back in time for the team meeting. Please, don't worry. How about I text you when I get there?"

"And when you're on the way back?" she insisted with a sad smile.

"Yes, on the way back too." I kissed her forehead, and she eased back down on the pillow. Dominic stirred in the bed. If I didn't leave now, I wouldn't. My little rascal liked playing with his father, and the feeling was mutual. I couldn't believe how much I loved being a father. I loved my family. I'd do anything to keep them safe.

I eased out of the room quietly and hurried to my SUV. The sun would be up soon. I could see slender fingers of light on the horizon. Soon it would banish the darkness altogether. But that wouldn't mean a hill of beans once we entered the cave. Inside the chambers, there would be nothing but inky blackness. As Butch warned us, we wouldn't be able to see our hands in front of our faces without a decent light source.

It didn't take long to reach the Cathedral Caverns State Park. I'd read up on the place so I wouldn't be surprised or blindsided by any strangeness. Before it got its swanky name, it used to be called Bat Cave—a fact I had not shared with Joshua, who hated the creatures. But nobody wanted to visit a park called Bat Cave, so the name was changed to Cathedral Caverns. The public had been visiting the place since the 1950s, but it wasn't a state park until 2000. From what I read, it had a massive entrance, a huge opening that may be a world record. Goliath Cave featured the Goliath, one of the largest stalagmites in the world. The entire cave system encompassed 493 acres. No way would we be covering all that ground.

The fact that gems were often found in the cave added to the narrative of lost riches. That's probably what kept people coming back to this location, the off chance of finding gemstones.

I swung my SUV into the parking lot. I saw no other vehicles, but there was an older gentleman standing by the gate. Pausing, I rolled down my window. "Mr. Jonas? I'm Midas Demopolis."

"Midas. Good. Let's take a walk together."

I glanced around as subtly as I could. I didn't sense danger, but that meant nothing. Danger comes in all shapes and sizes. I parked, still wondering about the early morning and the urgency. I grabbed my flashlight and phone to be prepared. Keys? Check. I got out and locked the truck. I was as ready as I'd ever be.

"Mr. Jonas, good morning. It is nice to meet you."

"Nice to meet you, Midas. I have read a lot of good reports about you and your team. Thank you for taking the time to come here." His smile appeared sad but sincere. It put me at ease, strangely enough.

"My pleasure, Mr. Jonas. My team and I are here to help you if we can."

"That's my hope. Well, we have a little way to walk, Midas, so we need to get started. You look healthy enough, though. This walk shouldn't be any problem for you."

"Yes, sir. I do like to stay in shape. Where is the center of the activity?"

"Mainly Goliath Cave, Midas. Follow me. We have to go deep into the cave system."

As we walked in silence, I breathed in the crisp morning air. The sun was breaking over the horizon now. It wouldn't matter. The massive opening in the ground offered no light. It was so large that it took my breath away. How could something that filled you with wonder be haunted?

Get your head in the game, Demopolis. You are not here to take in the magnificence of the place. You have a job to do. Time to focus.

"Mr. Jonas, how long have you been the caretaker here?"

"A long time, Midas, a long time. It's time for someone else to know about the goings-on here. My time at the Cathedral Caverns is coming to an end. This is the last thing I wanted to take care of before I leave. I can't leave knowing so many things are unknown."

"Tell me about what kind of things are happening and how my team can best help you."

"We have reports of knocking sounds. The miners call them Tommyknockers. There was one report of a young person going missing in Goliath Cave about fifteen or so years ago. They never found the body of the young man. Supposedly, there was a group of teens poking around in here, searching for gemstones. He—his name was Tony—got separated from the rest of the group, and nobody has seen him since. Very sad. People say they have heard the young man's voice calling for help." Mr. Jonas visibly shivered. "Also, we have had reports of a dark shadowy presence seen in the deepest parts of the cave system. Just beyond Goliath Cave."

"Wow, you do have a lot of activity here. Will there be anyone here while we're investigating?"

"Midas, you have free run of the whole place for the next two days. Here are the keys to the park so that you can get in and can have access to the restrooms. The ticket booth has power, so if you need electricity..."

"We will. Thank you, Mr. Jonas. Lead the way, sir."

For the next hour, we toured the cave. To my surprise, the cave system had a dim lighting system, handrails, and directionals that guided guests safely through the caverns.

"Here's Goliath. See that stalagmite? It's called Goliath because it's one of the largest in the world."

"I see. That is amazing. What a wonder!"

Mr. Jonas smiled. "I think so too. This is as far as I go. I'm not as strong as I used to be."

"This is good, sir. Thank you for the tour. I hope we can get some answers for you."

"Thank you, Midas. I will be looking forward to hearing from you."

We made the long trek back to the front of the cave system, and then Mr. Jonas turned to me and shook my hand. I couldn't understand the sadness I saw on his face. I was sure there was more to the story than what he was telling me, but I wouldn't press him.

I walked to the SUV and got in. I glanced around but didn't see any other vehicles. I did see Mr. Jonas, though. Where was he walking to? The old man seemed to just fade off into the sunrise. He must have parked behind the welcome center.

That was a lot to take in, and me without any coffee yet. *Shoot, I forgot to call Cassidy when I got here. Better do it now and beg forgiveness for my forgetfulness.*

"Hey, Cassidy. Sorry I didn't call when I got here. Mr. Jonas was already at the gate. I could tell he was a bit anxious and not one for wasting time."

"It's okay, Midas, I went back to sleep when you left. How did your meeting go?" She yawned as she snuggled with Dominic. I could hear him slurping on his bottle.

"It went very well. We had a great talk, and he shared a couple of stories. One about a missing teen. Something didn't seem completely right. I got the feeling that Mr. Jonas was holding something back, but it could be me overthinking everything."

"Trust your gut, Midas. It has never been wrong. You on your way back to the hotel?"

"Yes, I am leaving now. See you in about twenty minutes. I will come to help you with Dominic. We can go down to breakfast together."

"Good. I'll need help so I can get dressed. Your son is so needy this morning." She laughed softly. "I will see you soon. Be careful. Goodbye."

"Bye, honey." I hung up the phone and drove toward the hotel. The team was going to be excited about this case. I clicked off the recorder and put it on the seat beside me. I just remembered that I had it rolling.

Suddenly, I got the feeling that I wasn't alone. I tried to pretend that I didn't sense anything, but I couldn't resist looking over my shoulder.

Nothing. There was nobody there. Not a soul.

Just a nagging feeling that something was wrong.

I'd felt like this before, back at the Leaf Academy.

Nah, Midas. You're being paranoid. You'll never meet an entity like that again. Never. This case is nothing like that one.

Or so I prayed...

Chapter Three—Sierra

Joshua kissed me in the elevator. He had a thing about making out in elevators. Such a weirdo, but I loved it. Joshua was nothing if not a risk-taker. I had to promise him that we'd take an elevator ride later. Hopefully, we wouldn't get busted. I smiled at him as we walked into the hotel dining room. The smell of bacon and maple syrup made my stomach growl.

I never ate breakfast at home—who had the time? But when we were on the road, I couldn't resist. Breakfast was always better when somebody else cooked it. At least that was my theory. When I could twist his arm, Joshua whipped up a mean stack of pancakes. He didn't do that much anymore. The poor guy worked his behind off for us. But then again, so did I. Chasing after a toddler and Bozo, our rowdy dog, I never had any energy anymore.

I spotted the team easily enough. Butch, Jericho and Macie were already sitting at a large round table. A carafe of coffee and a glass jar of orange juice were already there. Yum! I couldn't wait.

"Hey, guys. Good morning!" I greeted the team as I took a seat by Macie.

She smiled and said, "Hey, Sierra, Joshua. I'm starving. Where's the boss and Cassidy? Should we wait for them?"

I glanced at my watch. It was already eight o'clock. It wasn't like Midas and Cassidy to be late, but then again, life with a small baby was always unpredictable. I knew that well enough. Babies laughed at schedules and their parents' plans. Babies were always the wild card.

"I'm sure they are on the way down. What's looking good on the menu?" I asked Macie as we studied it together. Nobody wanted to order until Midas and Cassidy joined us, but my stomach continued to complain. Well, I'd have to drink coffee to put it to rest. I hated drinking coffee on an empty stomach. After a few minutes of impatiently waiting, I texted Midas.

He didn't text me back. Instead, he and Cassidy walked into the dining room. Dominic was bright-eyed and bushy-tailed, looking all around. Such a handsome little fellow with his dark eyes and dark hair. Poor Cassidy. The baby looked nothing like her.

I rose from the table and went to retrieve my "nephew." "Dominic gets to sit by Aunt Si Si. Hey, little guy. Look, Joshua. Isn't he precious?" I said as I set his carrier down and unstrapped him. Scooping him up in my arms, I breathed him in. Oh, I loved that sweet baby smell. Gosh, I missed Emily being this small. Not enough to have another baby right now, though. I think Joshua was much more eager to grow our family than I was, but not always. He went back and forth on the subject, whereas I never changed my mind. It would take a lot for me to have another baby right now. Or in the next five years.

To my surprise, Joshua gave me the side-eye. "Don't get any ideas, Sierra Kay. One is enough."

"Tell yourself that, Joshua McBride. I'll just borrow Dominic occasionally if his mommy doesn't mind," I joked with him.

Cassidy handed me his pacifier. Dominic liked to suck constantly. He was a growing boy. "Anytime, Aunt Si Si, but I get Emily once in a while too. You never let her come over."

"I thought you had your hands full with Dominic. She would love to come see this little man. Isn't he gorgeous, Macie? Do you want to hold him? I warn you, babies are addictive."

Macie shook her head politely. "I have never held a baby. I wouldn't know how, and I think you need a partner for that. Taking care of Sherman is enough of a challenge for me. I can't go anywhere without him following me around. Even to the bathroom. I know it's not the same thing, a dog and a baby. But I'll be honest—I'm afraid I'd hurt Dominic because I'm so dang clumsy. Sherman is clumsier than I am."

Cassidy laughed sweetly. "I felt the same way until I had Dominic. What are we ordering, guys? I'm starving. I thought Midas would never get back."

Midas shot her a look. I didn't know what that meant, but I knew it couldn't be good. Clearly, Big Brother was keeping secrets. I wanted to drill him with questions, but the waitress arrived and Butch was already ordering. Jericho was quiet too.

Hmm...I guess his crush on Macie wasn't going as smoothly as he hoped. Stop, Sierra. No reading your friends. That's being nosy.

I tucked the pacifier back in Dominic's busy mouth and ordered pancakes and sausage. After everyone ordered, Midas asked Butch to share some pointers on cave safety. It wasn't anything I didn't expect to hear: Use the buddy system. Stay together. Follow only marked trails. Check your radios every hundred feet. The deeper you go, the fainter the signal. But hearing Butch's prompts reminded me how unsafe this could be if we weren't careful. Yeah, he was right to tell us to be safe. I didn't claim to be any cave aficionado.

Butch continued to talk. His blue eyes were focused and sharp as he studied each one of us. "Please, be careful. I know this cave system. There are surprises in there. The Cathedral Caverns are exactly why I started caving. As a teenager, my friends and I would come here in hopes of finding gems. And partying. Which I know now was a stupid idea. Caves have a certain magic to them, but they are extremely dangerous. Even well-traveled caves can hold surprises."

"What kind of surprises?" Jericho asked as he began pouring syrup on his waffles.

"Unknown crevasses. Cave collapses. Rock falls. The list goes on. Mind your Ps and Qs. Keep your lights on. Do regular radio checks. Stick together. Those are the most important things."

Midas nodded in agreement. "I got a call this morning from Mr. Jonas. He asked me to come and walk the cave with him."

"What? I thought I was going with you," I said sourly. I didn't mean to sound so snotty, but this wasn't how we operated. Or what we planned. Changes in schedules did not sit well with me.

"I know, I know. But he's the client, and he wanted a solo walk with me. It's no big deal. Don't worry, Little Sister. I recorded the whole thing. You didn't miss anything. Everything I heard, you will hear too." Midas shook his head and grinned at me.

He knew me so well. I had an insatiable need to know everything that had to do with Gulf Coast Paranormal. Some might call me a control freak, but really, I just wanted to stay on top of things. Planning was my forte. I mean, I had been the interim boss for quite a while. Had Midas forgotten that? And I'd been the office manager for a long time before that. I wasn't trying to be a hard-ass, but still. I liked to know. He could have called me. Or something.

I accepted the voice recorder and stuffed it in my pocket to keep it from getting wet. Or sticky. There was plenty of syrup on this table. Always protect the equipment. On more than one occasion, we'd captured an amazing EVP and then lost it due to something breaking.

"Hand me the baby, Sierra. I'm not super-hungry," Cassidy said as she held her hands out with a smile. I carefully deposited her bundle of joy in her arms and turned to my plate.

"Okay, but just say the word if you need me. Midas, what did Mr. Jonas say? What kind of vibe did you get from him?"

Midas sipped his coffee and glanced down at Dominic, who fussed for a moment. "I'm not as good with vibes as you are, Sierra. He seemed like a nice man. Genuinely concerned about the people who visit his cave. He sounded heartbroken about the missing teenager; his body was never found. But it's all on that tape."

Jericho paused between two bites. "You mean someone disappeared in the cave? Could that be the reason for the haunting?"

Midas confessed that he didn't really know. My mind immediately thumbed through my mental files. Yeah, I'd done quite a bit of research on the cave, but I'd somehow missed this tidbit. Now I really couldn't wait to review the digital recorder.

Butch broke the silence. "I remember that kid. Tony was his name. Tony Winchester. We used to hang out together quite a bit in high school. Not like best pals, but we ran in the same circles for a while. The whole town was shaken up when he disappeared. But like I told the cops, he left the cave. He was with Ashley. They walked out together. At least, I assumed they did. They'd been all over each other all night. I didn't see either one of them again."

"Wow, I didn't know that. Butch, are you sure you are up to this?" I asked with some concern. "You say you didn't know him very well?"

"Not as well as you'd think. Tony was a quiet kid. Until he fell in love. Ashley kind of brought him out of himself. She liked to pick fights, like a lot of teenagers do. Yes, I do want to go back. You guys need me, and maybe he does too. I still believe he left the cave. I mean, the idea that he got lost in there or got hurt... I don't want to believe that. I need to be there in case you get into a climbing situation."

"Agreed. We need your expertise, and now with this personal element, it's even more crucial that you are there, I think." Midas kissed his son's sleeping forehead again and sipped his coffee. "As far as other activity, it is what you would expect in a cave. Tommyknockers, strange shadows, voices. I think the client just wants to put his mind at ease. He plans to retire soon and wants to be sure it's safe for everyone who visits."

Even as he said that, I felt a creepy feeling along my spine. Everyone else must have felt the same strangeness because the crew got quiet. Maybe now would be the time to take a listen to the interview. I pulled the recorder out of my pocket and turned the volume down. I clicked play and held it up to my ear. I didn't want the entire restaurant to hear, but I was curious to see what Mr. Jonas had to say. Macie leaned closer to me. She was curious too, I guess.

The audio didn't start immediately, but finally, I heard Midas loud and clear. I turned up the volume a little bit. Yes, there was Midas again, only louder. I waited and waited, but there was no evidence that anyone else was with him. Macie frowned at me. Her eyes narrowed as I turned up the volume a bit. I cued the recording back and forth but couldn't hear the client at all.

"Where did you have the recorder, Midas? In your bag? In your back pocket?" I asked jokingly before switching it off with a frustrated sigh.

"No, in my hand. Why?"

"There's nobody on here. Just you," Macie said in a quiet voice. And she was right. The only voice on the device was Midas'.

There could be a few explanations. "Was he too far away? Were you guys deep in the system?" No, that wouldn't explain it, but it would make me feel better. If we could hear Midas, we should be able to hear Mr. Jonas.

"He was just a few feet away. Seriously. I had the volume turned all the way up, in my hand. Mr. Jonas knew I had it and agreed to being recorded. He wasn't whispering."

Jericho scratched his head. "So..."

What the heck was going on?

Chapter Four—Midas

We pulled up to the gate, and I gave the keys to Jericho to unlock it. He jumped out of the SUV, and I pulled in and parked. It was late morning, and we wanted to get set up and get the lay of the land. I needed time for the team to take in the beauty and dangers of the Cathedral Caverns so they could then focus on the task at hand. We didn't need to let this job get out of control. My plan was for us to focus on Goliath Cave and then span out according to whatever activity we witnessed.

"Joshua, we have power from the ticket booth for the monitors and whatever equipment you need to have a direct line to electricity. So set up as close as you can to Goliath Cave, which is the opening on the right. Do you think we have enough extension cords?" I shouldn't micromanage (we had Sierra for that), but I wanted to be sure.

"I sure do, Midas. I packed a couple extra hundred-foot cords before we left Mobile. I figured we'd need them for this investigation. I think I packed everything we had."

I patted him on the shoulder. I should never have doubted him. "Have Jericho and Macie help you get everything wired. Sierra, Butch and I are going to walk up to the entrance of Goliath Cave and form a plan to get started."

Joshua grinned at me. I could see the excitement on his face. I smiled back at him.

"Jericho, you still have the keys?"

"Sure do. Do you need them?" The young black man dangled them between us.

"No, you keep them to lock up tonight when we leave. Just don't lose them. One less thing for me to think about."

Sierra, Butch and I made our way to the entrance of Goliath Cave. Who was I fooling? I was still awestruck at the magnificence of the entrance even more now. We stopped at the entrance to discuss the details of the investigation. Sierra wanted to use a laser grid. Butch checked the perimeter for hidden slips, crevasses that someone could fall into.

"Nothing much has changed in here. Even after all these years," Butch mused to himself. After a moment, he got still and stood up straight, as if he heard something. "Midas, did you hear that?" Butch whispered, but even his whispers echoed in the cave.

I shook my head. "What was it, Butch? What did it sound like?"

"Knocking sounds coming from deep inside the cave. Further back. Could have been geological, but then again, it was pretty rhythmic."

I paused and tuned in also, but I didn't hear a thing. "Sierra, did you hear anything?"

"No, I did not. I did experience a cold chill for a split second, the kind I get when I make contact. But it didn't last long enough for me to pick up anything specific."

Interesting. We were experiencing activity already. What should we expect as the day wore on? *No matter, we have a job, and we must be about it.* Echoes would be a problem if we weren't careful. We'd have to take those into account. We brainstormed ideas but generally settled on what we'd planned before we arrived. The acoustics would be a challenge, but we'd make it work. I still had no explanation for why the client's voice didn't turn up on the audio recording.

"Sierra, I want you and Joshua to take baseline readings at the entrance of Goliath Cave. Have Jericho and Macie watch the monitors and man the radios."

She reached for her radio. "Don't forget Macie has Sherman. She promises to keep him on his leash."

Shoot. I forgot about the dog. "Sherman? That's fine. He can hang out with Jericho and Macie. Oh, and Sierra, tell the rest of the team they can head out as soon as you finish the baseline readings. Butch, be sure to grab the climbing gear just to be on the safe side."

"Sure thing, Midas."

Am I being too cautious or overthinking everything? No matter what, I want to keep this team safe. They are my family. Family looks after family. I cannot endure the loss of another family member. About twenty minutes later, the team was beginning to gather around. Now was the time to be me. Again. Time to be Midas.

"Okay, guys, this is Goliath Cave, the focal point of our investigation tonight. Amazing, huh? I have been telling you about this place, but it's hard to describe. As with all caves, this one is dimly lit, so be careful of your footing. Stay together! No one goes off alone, Joshua."

He shrugged good-naturedly. "What?"

"Butch and I will go into Goliath first. Sierra and Joshua will move to the front of the caverns to take baseline readings near the entrance. Follow any leads, but you must check in with Macie before you go off. We need to always keep track of everyone. This place is massive, and the tunnels have tons of twists and turns. It would be easy to get turned around. The marked-off areas are a no-go, people. No stepping over chains or ducking under gates. Jericho and Macie will sweep the monitors for the first hour. Let's check in every fifteen minutes with the radios. Safety is a priority. No risks!"

After a radio check, we headed out to our specified locations. Butch and I made our way back down the path into Goliath Cave. He was keenly aware of the sounds that he heard earlier. The path was truly dimly lit and a bit slick. The handrail gave me some peace of mind but not a lot as we descended.

Butch seemed to be on edge as we headed deeper into the cave. I didn't know whether it was flashbacks to the last time he was here, or the possibility of finding gemstones, or that he was really wanting to impress me with his attentiveness. Gosh, I hated being so cynical. I had no reason not to trust Butch. None at all.

He suddenly raised his hand in a fist. "Midas, there it is again. Knocking. Repeated knocking."

I thought maybe I heard something, but I couldn't be sure. "Which direction, Butch?"

"Same as earlier. Deeper in the system. That way." He pointed ahead of us.

I reached for my radio. "Macie, this is Midas." I wanted to make sure the cameras were going back here.

"Yes, Midas. I hear you loud and clear."

"Are the cameras rolling in Goliath? Have you seen anything on the monitors? Butch keeps hearing knocking ahead of us."

Macie paused as if she were talking with Jericho. "We haven't seen anything here, but we'll keep watch. We're on it."

I tapped on the radio. "Copy that. We are going to continue into the depths of Goliath Cave." I decided to check in with Sierra too. "Come in, Sierra, this is Midas."

Her perky voice came back almost immediately. "Go ahead, Midas, this is Sierra."

"Anything happening at the entrance? How are those baselines looking? We're about to deploy the light grid in here."

"Nothing yet, Midas, all readings are normal. No high EMF. Nothing."

Well, what did I expect? We'd only begun our investigation. "Okay. Headed deeper into the cave. I've got my GoPro lit and rolling."

"Great, Midas."

Daylight began to fade away as we continued down. I wasn't one to get claustrophobia, but the walls seemed to close in on me. Even in this large cavern. Shadows began to grow, but that's what happened in dark places. And shadows could play tricks on your eyes. Butch was still on his toes as we continued on. Man, this place was huge.

I noticed him constantly looking over the edge at each drop-off. Maybe he was trying to be aware, I didn't know. Occasionally he'd say, "Watch your step here."

I paused momentarily. What was that sound? Was it water dropping, or were these the knocking sounds Butch heard earlier? So many sounds in here. Lots and lots of sounds. As if the Goliath had come alive. Definitely not water droplets.

Knock. Knock. Knock.

"Hey, Butch. Take a listen." Were these the knocking sounds that Mr. Jonas was talking about? The old miners say they are warning signs of impending rock fall. But I didn't see any loose rocks in here.

Knock. Knock. Knock.

"It's not me, Midas. It sounds like someone is banging on a pipe. I'm right next to you. Do you think I could pull that off with you right here?"

He was right, of course. "Hey, I didn't say it was you, Butch. Let's settle down and wait. Whatever or whoever is in here knows we're here. Let's watch the grid."

"Sorry. It's this place, Midas. I guess coming back here hit me worse than I expected. Good idea. I'll set a digital recorder out too. Just in case we get some EVPs."

I gave him a thumbs-up. "We may as well hunker down, then. Hopefully, they're getting these noises on the cameras." The knocks had stopped momentarily, but I was hopeful that they would resume.

"Hopefully so. Now is the fun part." I smiled in the dark as I turned off my headlamp. Butch did the same.

"Yeah, what's the fun part?"

"Waiting. It's always the fun part."

41

We didn't have long to wait.

Chapter Five—Sierra

Joshua and I walked slowly along the front of the cavern. My hiking boots crunched the brittle rocks beneath me. How old was this place? Thousands of years? Tens of thousands? There was really no telling. I was certainly not a geologist. You know, this was a question I could get an answer for, though. I mean, I was a damn good researcher.

Midas didn't know it, but I'd dug up information about that kid Tony. The one that disappeared back when Butch was exploring the place. A local kid with a big smile. Well-liked, by all accounts, but it didn't seem like the local police department had done much to try to find him. A two-day search and then nothing? If I'd been his parents, I would have been pretty upset about the way the cops handled this case.

Joshua put his hand out toward me. I paused, but I heard it too. That old familiar feeling of walking into spider webs struck me. Naturally, I wiped my hand across my face, but I knew it was no spider and no spider web. My paranormal feelers were going off, but I had no idea where it was coming from. Joshua took my hand as if he wanted to protect me, but from what?

Clack, clack, clack, clack, clack.

It was getting louder and closer.

"What the hell? Is that a mine car? Do they have those in here?" I couldn't be sure, but something was certainly barreling toward us. God, it was so close! The ground reverberated beneath my shoes. The rocks rattled too. Joshua held on to me as we waited to see what approached. Was this an earthquake? Holy crap! We needed to run!

"Move, Sierra Kay!" Joshua slung me across the passageway and practically fell on top of me. The clacking had gotten louder, and the car, or whatever it was, blasted past us.

I swore like a sailor as my heart pounded dangerously in my chest. What was this? I clutched my husband's shoulders and stared into his eyes. His lips were set grimly, but he held my gaze. It was all I needed to stay grounded, to keep from completely losing it. The cringy touch of ectoplasm hit me again, but I could do nothing to prevent it. An image flashed in my mind, a terrible picture of a grinning face with black teeth and empty eyes.

In a few seconds, it was all over. All of it. I panted for breath as Joshua heaved off me. He helped me to my feet before dusting off his knees. Where had the thing gone? My hands were shaking, my body trembling. I waved my flashlight's beam on the ground.

"Joshua? What just happened?"

"It was a mine car. A phantom mine car."

Neither one of us asked the obvious question. How could that have been a mine car? There were no rails? Nothing for a mine car to ride on.

"Joshua, look." I squatted down and rubbed my hands along the floor of the cave. "There is no rail. Nothing at all. If there was a mine car in here, it was a long time ago. They must have removed the rail to keep everyone safe. Where did it go?" I was so excited, I barely noticed how pale he appeared. "Hey, are you okay?"

"Did you see the guy? Did you see what was in it?" Joshua was shaken up. I had seen the being, but only in my mind's eye. Not like he had, apparently, and I told him as much. He was reaching for my radio. I handed it to him. "Josh for Midas."

After a few seconds, Big Brother answered the call. "Go for Midas."

"We just had some crazy activity. Can you join Sierra and me? We just...I just saw an apparition. A full-fledged apparition."

45

"Where are you at?"

"Between C and E. Past the ticket booth toward you."

"On the way."

Joshua radioed Macie next. "Hey, guys. Did you catch anything on camera? We're in the tunnel between C and E. I don't think there are any cameras set up in this section, but I thought I'd check. Sierra and I... well, something just happened. I'm praying that you caught it. Some kind of way."

"Checking." After a brief pause, she answered, "I have about five seconds of fuzz at the entrance of C. Jericho is rolling it back to make sure. I'll get back to you. Give us a few minutes. You guys okay?"

"Yeah, we're fine."

As we waited, Joshua paced the small space. He too examined the floor for evidence of a mine car, but there were no recent signs of anything like that. We took readings with our EMF detector, but there were only occasional faint hits. Point seven. Point eight. Then back to zero. Flat. Whatever that had been had taken a lot of energy to scare us. Or warn us.

Or something.

"Tell me what you saw, Josh."

"I saw the mine car as it rushed past us. But it didn't go down this way." He waved his arm toward the direction from which Midas and Butch were walking up. "It went through the wall. Over there. I even felt the damn wind blow. It's like this cave wall wasn't even here. And there was a guy in it. He had on a hat, an old-fashioned denim cap with a strange sort of lamp on it. His face was terrifying."

"What did he look like? Could it have been Tony?"

"No, I don't think so. I saw an old man. He had the look of an emaciated prisoner of war. Almost a skeleton. I would call him a corpse except for the fact he turned his head toward us and stared at me. He was here and gone in a matter of seconds."

"You're joking, Joshua. Seriously? You saw that much detail? It is pretty dark down here. Maybe your eyes are just matrixing? Trying to make something out of the shadows?"

"Give me a break, Sierra Kay. You know I'm not the kind of guy that makes up shit. I know what I saw. I don't know why I saw it. That's your job, seeing things. Help me look around. Maybe it is a trick or a gimmick of some sort."

Wow, that stung. What was eating him? Joshua had been kind of on edge since we got here. I should have taken him on the elevator ride when I had the chance. It might have helped his nervous attitude this afternoon.

By the time we finished examining the tunnel, Midas and Butch joined us, as did Macie, Jericho and Sherman. The large white dog was not happy about the harness and leash he was currently wearing. I take it he didn't normally wear such a getup. As soon as he joined us, he got to sniffing the ground.

Good. Maybe he would find something that would lead us to more evidence. I squatted down and petted the big, friendly dog. He loved me. I had been his foster mom for a while when Jocelyn died, but I never brought that up.

Midas had his usual worried expression. Too worried. "You guys feeling alright? On the way here, Butch pointed out that there can be pockets of gas in here. Some of these gases can cause hallucinations. Did you smell anything weird before you heard the clacking?"

Joshua frowned at him like he had two heads. "I didn't smell anything, and I wasn't hallucinating. I heard the damn thing before it got here. So did she. It smashed into the wall, with a freaking skeleton-looking dude in it, and then vanished. End of story."

Wow. My husband was definitely on edge. Definitely afraid. So not like Joshua McBride. I needed to remind him that we were fine. That this is what we do.

"We've already searched the tunnel for evidence of a rail. We found nothing, but I know what I heard. I heard a mine car. I heard it crashing into the wall. I only saw kind of a blur because Joshua pushed me out of the way. He was trying to protect me. Hey, Macie! Did you guys find anything?"

"Yeah, we got it. Jericho, where's the iPad? This man is brilliant! It's only a small clip, but we caught a glimpse."

Jericho whipped out the tablet and tapped on it. He spun it around with a bright smile on his face. "Check it out," he said with a wave of his hand.

Midas accepted the tablet, and we all hovered around him to see. The footage was great, better than I expected in these caves. There was Joshua and me—and then I paused. We both held our breath. That must have been the moment we heard the cart approaching. I saw Joshua shove me out of the way and a white blur whiz past us. Between us. And just like Joshua said, the blur vanished on the other side of the cave. I didn't see a skeleton or any kind of apparition, but I did see the shape of the cart. Or something.

"No audio?" Midas asked in his most serious voice.

"Nope. And we can't explain that because the audio is running." Jericho's bright smile vanished. "Sorry about that."

"No apologies necessary. This is great evidence. So strange, though. I don't recall Mr. Jonas mentioning anything about a mine car. Well, let's hang out here a little longer. Deploy some REM pods. See if we can draw it out again."

After about an hour, we gave up. It was time to move on to other parts of the cave. One thing was for sure, I would be thinking about that experience all night. And beyond.

I wondered what it meant. Was the guy in the cart trying to hurt us? Was he trying to warn us? Hmm...I'd have to do more research on this once we got out of this cave. Yeah, I didn't like it here. I didn't like it at all.

"Sierra Kay, stay close to me. Okay? No arguing." Joshua's voice sounded sharp and serious. His mood had soured since the experience, even more so than earlier. I had questions, but now wasn't the time to interrogate him.

"Got it. I'll stay close." I accepted his hand, and the group of us headed back to the ticket booth. I was glad to be moving toward the front of the cave. The closer we got to the booth, the easier it was to breathe. Was I okay?

I glanced up at Joshua. His tanned face appeared pale too. He didn't like this either. I could tell. I knew my husband. Better than anyone else. I loved him. Whatever he was going through, I hoped he knew he could come to me. I would be here for him. If he let me. I mean, he'd already experienced so much with his parents' divorce and his new position at work. More responsibility. Not much more money.

Jericho played the video of Joshua and me on the large monitor. While they did that, I plugged in my earbuds and listened to the digital recorder. Just in case. About ten minutes in, while the team was still examining and reviewing the video, I caught the voice.

A young voice.

It sounded like a boy, but I couldn't be sure.

He was crying. Crying for someone. What was her name?

Yeah, I could almost make it out.

Ashley...why did you leave me?

Chapter Six—Midas

I could tell that Little Sister and Joshua were shaken up by the apparition of the man in the mine car. A skeleton man. This investigation was kicking off on a spooky note. I decided to give them a break and not question them for a few minutes so that they could regain their composure. I knew them to be competent investigators, but anyone could get shaken up under the right circumstances.

Been there, done that.

A dark, dank cave was certainly the right environment for letting your imagination run wild. The video evidence was amazing, though, and backed up their experience. Not that I needed confirmation. I believed them. I trusted them.

I had Josh and Sierra stay at the ticket booth while I moved Macie and Jericho near the cave entrance. The McBrides agreed to let Sherman hang out with them. Macie and Jericho did not seem happy about that. They wanted to investigate between C and E and see what Sierra and Joshua had witnessed. But so many events were taking place. This was too much, too soon.

Safety was important. Much more important than running off half-cocked.

What was going on in this cave, and what had happened to create so much residual energy? Yeah, that's what I was feeling. Residual energy.

Better do a radio check. Stay connected to your people. I suddenly missed Cassidy. Yeah, it wasn't the same without her by my side.

I walked away from Macie and Jericho. They were complaining but only to each other. Good. The change of location wasn't something I was going to argue about. They needed to trust me.

I needed to trust me. I headed back to Goliath. Butch had gathered his climbing equipment, and we planned to look for holes, possible gaps where someone might fall.

"Come in, Sierra. Do you hear me?" The radio crackled momentarily but cleared up quickly. Her voice came back nice and clear.

"Sierra here. We hear you loud and clear."

"Come in, Macie. Radio check."

"This is Macie. Jericho and I hear you loud and clear." She didn't sound any happier with me, but I ignored the disappointment in her voice.

"Okay, team. Butch and I are moving to the back of the cave to set up the laser grid and camera equipment. Let's do a radio check in thirty minutes."

"Got you, Midas," Sierra answered in her most professional voice. She wasn't fooling me, though. I could hear it in her tone. I wondered what they saw. Was it an apparition? From what the cameras had shown, something had indeed moved through. But to us, it appeared white and misty. Joshua had seen much more detail. He insisted that he did, and I believed that he had seen an apparition. Joshua McBride was no liar.

"Got you, Midas," Jericho responded. I could hear Macie wrestling with Sherman in the background. Was Sherman sensing something?

Butch and I continued our journey back to Goliath. The path was clear, but we still had to watch every step. There were tons of loose rocks everywhere. Every step we made, I heard rocks falling onto the path. Falling from where?

I scanned the ceiling with my flashlight. No, I didn't see any falling rocks. No loose spots.

Were the spirits telling us to stay out, or was it just the nature of the cave? As we reached the cavern, we began to deploy the light grid. It only took a minute or two. The equipment worked beautifully. I scurried to the other side of the cave to focus the camera on the grid. If anything moved in front of the lights, we would all see it. Even though we had activity in the tunnel between C and E, I still felt compelled to stick to Goliath. I couldn't say why.

I noticed Butch squatting on the ground to the right of the light grid. He'd reached for his Maglite and was shining it down, but I did not see anything. Where was the light going?

"Found something. Come check this out, Midas."

I tapped on the camera one last time and then carefully went to join Butch. He was leaning over a crack. No, an opening. It wasn't very large, just big enough for a smaller guy to get through. Butch being the cave dog he was, I knew he wanted to go down and examine it for himself.

"Are you thinking what I'm thinking?" He grinned at me as he slid off his backpack.

I laughed as I squatted down next to him. "I doubt it."

He handed me his flashlight as he pulled out a bundle of cord. "I have to check this out. Could be something. Could be nothing. Looks big enough. There's no telling what's down here. I was here a dozen times as a young man, and I have never seen this fissure. This could be dangerous if we don't map it for Jonas."

He had a point. We couldn't just let this go unreported. Yeah, we needed to check this out. *Here I am, breaking my own rules and doing everything I told myself I would not do. This wasn't what we planned. Wait until I tell Sierra.*

"Okay, Butch. You go down and check it out, but I want a safety line attached to you so I can pull you back. Just in case of emergency. I mean, you really don't know what's down there." What was I thinking?

"Gotcha. No problem. I will be careful and stay in touch by radio." I could hear the excitement in his voice. These adventurers were crazy—but then again, people said that about me too. He took his time and hitched up to his safety gear.

I radioed Sierra. "Can you see us on the camera?"

"Yeah, I see you. What are you doing?"

I waved at the camera. "If you can see us, you already know."

I heard her sigh. "Go slow, guys."

"Roger that."

With some trepidation, I watched as Butch rappelled down into the darkness and into the unknown. A rope and a radio were his only connection to me. My nerves were beginning to surface.

Hadn't I told myself that I would never put myself in this situation again? But here we were. There really was no way to prevent this. I had to trust that Butch knew what he was doing. They all did. Why was I worried? We were all professionals, right?

"Okay, Butch, take your time. Do not take any chances." I tried to hide the hesitancy in my voice. My mind summoned up images of Jocelyn falling from the roof. Her eyes wide, her hands reaching for me. I couldn't help but close my eyes to clear my head.

"Gotcha, Boss. This is in my wheelhouse." Into the crevasse he went. Yeah, I was excited but also worried. Butch said he'd never seen this spot before. That seemed odd. We weren't too far off the beaten path. No matter what, the investigation must continue.

"Butch? What can you see?" I didn't hear anything for a few seconds.

Breathe deep, Midas.

Finally, he answered me. "It's a big space. I can't believe I've never seen this before."

"Do you see anything?" I wasn't necessarily asking if he saw a skeleton or a chest of jewels. Just anything. The atmosphere up here was changing. No. Not the air but the way it felt in here. The electricity. "Are you safe down there?" I was getting worried. I had the sweats.

"Yeah. It looks like it opens to a larger room about ten feet from here. Making my way there now."

Wow. Okay. Keep it together, Midas. "Great! Do you have your GoPro rolling?"

"Turning it on now. Sorry, Boss."

I radioed Sierra. "Hey, Lil Sis. Butch has his GoPro going. Hit record, okay?"

"Yep, and I'm pulling him up now. Wow. That looks freaking amazing. There are literally lights everywhere. What, Joshua? Oh, excuse me. Not lights but pieces of stones."

A few minutes passed. I radioed Butch again. Radio silence wasn't acceptable in a situation like this. But there was nothing but static on the radio and no response from Butch. He normally responded immediately. I didn't peg him for a cowboy. This wasn't the time for that. Joshua made sure everyone had new batteries in all their equipment, from GoPros to digital recorders. I was sure of that.

Suddenly, the rope tightened as if something was pulling on it. I swore under my breath. Was it Butch? Was he in danger? I peered down but did not see Butch's flashlight. Or him, for that matter. I tightened my grip on the rope and tried calling him louder this time.

"Butch, come in! Butch, you need to answer me!"

I heard a cracking voice coming over the radio. "You can't...me? I'm.... Check ... place out. .... Midas." Relief flooded over me when I heard his voice. Still, I was a bit ticked. Time to call this part of the investigation.

"Butch come back up," I commanded as I tried to hide the worried tone in my voice.

His broken voice came back over the radio. "Midas, I see .... at the edge of my .... Let ... check ... out."

"No, Butch. Come back to the opening. I need to put eyes on you. No more solo runs." Yeah, I had to put my foot down. I couldn't do this again.

"Roger, Boss," Butch answered, with clear disappointment in his voice. A few minutes later, he came up from the small opening; he was covered head to toe with dust. "We have to go back. There's a feeling down there. Not just your average in-a-dark-cave sensation. Also, there's evidence of gems in the rocks."

"What kind of gems?" I asked stubbornly. I wasn't going to change my mind on this; he needed to stay connected to the team. Going off radio was not an option.

Butch couldn't hide his excited smile. "Like actual treasure. Can you believe it? Gems are embedded in that far wall. Not only that, I saw what looked like a pair of boots, but I can't be sure. I couldn't get close enough. It was too far from the opening."

"How far away are we talking?" I asked, curious now.

"Another fifty feet."

Regardless, it would have to wait for another time. I knew what he was hoping—to finally put to rest the questions surrounding Tony's disappearance. I wanted that too, but we needed to do it properly.

"Let's set up the REM pod and do an EVP session."

He nodded as he unhooked himself from his harness. "You know we have to check that out, Midas. You know we have to."

"I know. We will, but Jericho is going down with you. No one goes alone. You know that, and you know why." I didn't want to mention Jocelyn's name, but I would if I had to. His eyes said it all. Of course he understood. He knew exactly what I was talking about. Butch and I began setting the equipment up. I was hoping to get evidence to put Mr. Jonas' mind at ease. Not add to the problem by losing a team member. I shivered at the thought.

I needed to check in with the team. "Sierra? This is Midas. Do you hear me?" Nothing. I radioed her two more times. What was going on with these radios? Was I overreacting?

Little Sister's voice broke through my worried thoughts. "Midas? Do you hear me?"

"Yeah. You okay? How is everything at the booth?"

"Yes, everything is fine. You guys see or hear anything?"

I wasn't ready to move on from this conversation. "Sierra, I have called you three times."

"I only heard you the one time, Midas. What's up?"

Before I could tell her what I really thought, a shadow figure broke the light grid and the REM pod went off.

Jesus! What was that?

"Hold on, Sierra. We are getting some activity," I whispered to her and Butch. "I will radio you back in a moment."

"Okay," she said as the radio clicked off.

I reached for the digital recorder and made sure the volume was turned up. "I saw you. What is your name? Are you a miner?"

Butch and I continued to work the session, making sure to pause between questions. After playing the recording back, we were even more frustrated. There was nothing to hear but us asking questions. Nothing but silence except for the REM pod, which was still going off every so often. Every now and then, we could see the light grid darken. We had to keep trying because we weren't alone.

"Can you tell me your name? We are not here to harm you."

Nothing but silence and all the equipment stopped performing. There were no lights moving, no EVPs.

A rock fell at my feet.

And then two more.

The last one "fell" hard and bounced off the tip of my boot. I hit the massive ceiling with my flashlight. Rocks weren't falling on Butch. *What gives?* Who or what was down here with us?

"Let's try something else, Midas. We need the FLIR, I think."

"Good idea." I shook my head. "Joshua, come in." I waited but heard nothing. "Damn it. Why isn't he responding? The radios are crapping out."

"Sierra, come in. Can you hear me?"

"Yes, I hear you."

I breathed a sigh of relief. "Where is Joshua? I am trying to reach him."

"He went to the van to get another monitor. This one isn't working. He has his radio. I don't know why he is not answering. Maybe it's the distance?"

"When you see him, tell him I need a FLIR camera. ASAP."

"I will, Midas. Is there anything that I can help with? Want me to bring it to you?"

Her chipper voice soothed my sudden anger. "No, stay put. Tell Joshua to radio me."

"Roger that, Midas."

I shook my head. Why was I feeling so frustrated? "Butch, let's start taking down the equipment and begin packing up. We will come back here tomorrow with a plan. I'll get Jericho to help you investigate the room you found."

"Packing up? Things are just getting cooking. I'm not in a hurry."

Even as he said that, we heard knocking sounds coming from all around us. Not one, not two but dozens of tapping sounds.

Rocks struck us. Small, stinging ones.

"Damn!" Butch said as he put his hand on his head. Obviously, he got whacked with a rock. "This ain't good."

The message was clear.

It was time to get out.

Now.

Chapter Seven—Joshua

I hoofed it back to the van. Macie and Jericho were still in the tunnel where my wife and I had our experience with the mine car. Why wouldn't Midas let us continue our investigation? He wasn't acting like the Midas that I knew. That we all knew.

I radioed Macie and Jericho on the way just to check on them. Also, I didn't want them to think I was a ghost. So far, I was impressed with the caves. The Cathedral Caverns were a beautiful geological landmark, but I'd never been one for caves. The activity was incredible. And building. Were we ready for it?

Luckily for me, the technical guy, we weren't canvassing the entire cave system, mainly Goliath Cave. Despite the geographical limitation, it was a tough gig to cover in a technical sense.

To be honest, I was glad the dang monitor went out. I needed to get out of there for a minute. I had an uncomfortable feeling. A smothering, uncomfortable feeling.

It wasn't one I associated with the usual paranormal cases, and there had been plenty of them. This had a different feel to it. A different uncomfortable feeling. It troubled me that I couldn't quite put my finger on it, and I didn't know how to talk about it with Sierra.

Or Midas. Or anyone.

I didn't like it in the cave, despite the natural beauty. I wasn't claustrophobic, not that I knew of, but I much preferred being outside under the stars. I wasn't excited about being here. I didn't know why. I hoped it would pass because if it didn't, I'd have to make some tough decisions.

Yeah, I was in a funk. That's all it was.

Maybe I was burned out. I was tired of lugging equipment, changing batteries, and fixing broken things. It was as if Midas forgot that I knew how to investigate. I felt like a rookie. A lackey. Unappreciated. There had to be more to this whole paranormal investigation thing than being the crew's battery go-to guy.

Cloudy skies limited my visibility, so I reached for my flashlight. Clicking it on, I headed to the van hoping I had indeed brought the cords that went to this monitor. I'd been forgetting things lately. Kind of absent-minded. I didn't know what to make of it.

Out of the corner of my eye, I thought I saw a figure. There were no other cars in the parking lot except for ours. Who the heck was this, and why was he hanging out by the van? The shadow dipped around behind the back of the van, or so I thought. Was someone trying to break into our vehicles? Steal equipment or steal the whole dang vehicle? The thought angered me.

"Hey! Who's there?" I pointed the flashlight toward the movement, but nobody answered me.

"Damn," I whispered to myself. I reached for my radio. Maybe I should call Midas. Or Jericho. Did I need backup?

Come on, McBride. You're jumping at shadows. After what you saw in the caverns, a shadow shouldn't make you flinch.

I shivered remembering the clacking of the mine car and the terrible skeletal face of the phantom that rode in it. I headed to the back of the van and waved the flashlight around.

"Hey!" I shouted as loud as I could. I guess I thought the loudness would scare the guy away.

There wasn't a soul around. I stalked around the van and then the SUV. There was nowhere for a person to hide. No trees, no buildings. Not out here. I even looked under the vehicles.

Okay, get moving. I need a monitor. That's it.

I unlocked the back of the van and climbed in. The van light flooded the vehicle, and I breathed a sigh of relief. It was good to be in the light, but I couldn't hang out here. I removed the black case that contained the monitor I needed. It had a high-res screen and was one of the newer ones.

I opened the case and verified that I had a power cord but not the specific one I needed. I mean, the one I left behind might work, but I couldn't be sure. I sure as heck didn't want to trek back and forth between the van and the ticket booth all night. Setting the radio and flashlight down on the shelf, I tapped my fingers on a nearby box.

Dang it. Why didn't I check this before we left?

This wasn't like me at all. I tore through a crate of cords, but then the van light dimmed momentarily. I glanced above me. Just a flicker, I hoped. We didn't need the van battery to go kaput. That's when I saw the guy again. No features, only a black figure except his dirty black shoes. Gravel cracked beneath his shoes before he turned away. No way did I imagine that! I got the feeling that it was the guy I'd seen in the cave.

The dead guy. The guy who crashed into the mine wall. The guy with the emaciated, skeletal-looking face. Had he followed me out here?

"Hey! What are you doing?"

I jumped out of the back of the van, a power cord still in my hand. Spinning around, waving the cord like a weapon, I didn't see a soul. *Okay, I call BS.* I knew there was someone checking me out. The shoes—I'd seen his shoes. But then again, I couldn't see his face. No face at all. He was all black, except for those greasy black shoes. I walked around the vehicles and the ground, but it was impossible to see tracks in gravel.

Where was my flashlight?

Suddenly, my radio squawked to life. Someone was calling my name!

"Joshua! Midas! Someone, come in!" The radio wailed and shrieked again. "Macie?"

Sierra! That was Sierra!

I forgot all about the monitor and the van and the shadow I'd been chasing. As fast as I could, I hurried back into the cave. I ran pell-mell until I entered the caverns. And then, everything melted away.

The dim electrical lights. The directional and welcome signs. Everything familiar vanished, and for a moment, I stood in a different place. It was still the caverns, but it had to be a different time. I heard the chipping of picks on rock. I heard men yelling at one another.

Stranger still, the energy had changed. It was charged with anger and despair and confusion. All of a sudden, three men were running toward me. They were covered in dirt and grease, and there were tools in their hands.

"Fire in the hole!" I heard someone screaming as the earth began quaking beneath me. What was happening? This wasn't right! Not at all.

No! Sierra! I have to get to Sierra!

Collapsing to my knees, I put my hands up to cover my face. I wanted to protect myself from the explosion and the men who ran toward me. As the explosion occurred, the wind got knocked out of me. I fell backwards, and the atmosphere shifted again.

I was back and gasping for air.

"Sierra," I tried whispering, but I still had no breath.

The cavern began spinning around me.

Chapter Eight—Cassidy

I patted my son's padded bottom gently as he snuggled up to my neck. This was love. True love. My heart melted as I kissed Dominic's cheek again. He smelled like baby lotion and milk and heavenly sweetness. Sierra was right. Despite their occasionally offensive diapers, babies were the sweetest things on earth. At least mine was, but then again, I was pretty partial. Before Dominic, the only baby I'd cared for was my kid sister, Kylie. She sure would have loved him.

I miss you, Kylie. I miss you and I love you.

I stood before the bathroom mirror to make sure my son wasn't playing possum. Dominic was only an infant, but he was an expert at playing possum. Gosh, I never knew I could love someone this deeply. He looked so much like his father with his dark hair and lashes.

Yep, he was out like a light. For the moment. The trick to getting a good night's sleep was laying him down without waking him up. Sometimes it went smoothly. Other times...not so much. Here in this strange hotel room, I hoped for the best.

I breathed a sigh of relief as I placed the baby in the center of the bed. Even though we were far from home, Dominic didn't seem to mind. He probably didn't understand he was away from home. I did feel guilty about leaving Domino behind, but managing him and Dominic would have been impossible. Cats didn't travel well. Especially mine. Domino still wasn't certain what he thought about our baby. My spoiled cat tended to avoid my son, but I was sure he'd come around. His curiosity would eventually get the best of him.

Domino had always been a good boy. A very good boy. My constant companion for so long. However, if I left him alone too long, he tore the house up. Dug the plants up, ripped curtains and whatever else he liked.

Oh well. There was nothing I could do about that. I had insisted on coming. Midas needed me, or so I wanted to believe. If I could use my skills for the team's benefit, I would. I studied Dominic a minute. He wasn't stirring, which was good, but a part of me wanted to climb into bed with him and snuggle. Which would defeat the purpose entirely. I needed to sketch, to connect with the other side.

My mind wandered a while, and I let it go where it wanted to. I couldn't force my creative sessions. All that would get me was frustration. The spirits would reach me when they got ready. Hopefully. And hopefully in time to help my Gulf Coast Paranormal family.

In the meantime, I washed my face and got ready for bed. After my shower, I rubbed my arms and hands with lotion. I always felt so dry, ever since the pregnancy. Sierra was right—again. Pregnancy changes the body. I peeked in on Dominic. He was still out. I sat on the comfy chair by the window. All the lights were out except for the bathroom light, which I'd leave on for Midas. Just a crack in the door. I didn't want him to come back to the room and trip over a bag. I flicked on the lamp and reached for my bag.

It didn't take long for the images to come. At least now the images did not overwhelm me. I had more control over how quickly they rolled into my mind. It was a good feeling to use my gift without allowing it to consume my life. My time in Greece had come with unexpected awareness. Was it the culture? The love and acceptance of the Demopolis family? Becoming a mother? I couldn't be sure, but I was grateful for it.

Scratch, scratch.

My pencil began gliding over the blank page. I loved the feel of graphite on paper. Normally, I sketched to music, but not tonight. Dominic would certainly wake up, and I didn't feel comfortable wearing my earbuds. What if he needed me? I raised up in the chair one more time to double check that he was okay. Yep. Perfectly fine.

Back to my work...scratch, scratch. A man...

I couldn't quite see him, but his sadness was unmistakable. Oh dear, he didn't want to show me his face. Well, I would at least sketch what I saw. Maybe that would be enough. With bold, definite strokes, I outlined the back of his head, his broad shoulders, his arms.

Tell me who you are. How can I help you? Let me see. I'm here to help.

My silent pleas went nowhere. I couldn't understand why. I knew the mystery man wanted help. He definitely wanted help. Instead of discovering more of his identity, I saw him walking.

Back and forth. To and fro. Always. Constantly. Forever.

My hands reached for a flat black pencil. I shaded the arches above him. A cave! Yes, he was definitely in a cave system. I drew a snapshot of one of his worn paths. Poor man. Trapped there. Always searching, but for what? Treasure? A way out?

Tell me. Let me help you.

He said nothing. He wouldn't even look at me. After a while, I put the paper and pencil down. I could see nothing else. I sighed, knowing I hadn't achieved all that I wanted. All that I needed. This was an incomplete sketch. Not enough information for the team. Not really. I studied it again, holding the tablet up to the lamp one more time. This was it. This was all I could see and all he would tell me. For now. Maybe he'd talk more tomorrow. Clearly, he wanted to communicate something to me. I needed to be patient.

I clicked off the light and put the sketchbook on the table. Heading off to the bathroom, I washed my hands and dried them. The trip was finally catching up with me. Time to get forty winks, if Dominic allowed that.

Quietly and carefully, I slid in the bed beside my son. I resisted the urge to kiss him again. My eyes studied him in the half-light until I couldn't keep them open anymore.

Sooner than expected, I fell into a deep sleep. I dreamed about nothing.

Chapter Nine—Midas

The SUV needed gasoline, but I was too tired to stop. In the morning, for sure. It had been a long night, but the investigation promised to be an interesting one. Finding Joshua passed out at the entrance of the cave had been terrifying. Thank God nothing major was wrong with my friend. He recounted his experience carefully and allowed us to record him. Joshua was no stranger to any of this, but this occurrence had apparently shaken him to the core.

Because of the event, we knew there had once been an explosion in the mine. For whatever reason, the men who died there—the trio that didn't make it—out wanted Joshua to see them. To know they were there. The fact that it had affected him physically was shocking. By the time we'd gotten him back on his feet and rounded up Sherman, it was getting late.

Sierra's panic over the escaped animal had set us to running through the caves. Thank goodness we found him. I can't say what Macie would have done if we hadn't rescued him. I hoped she left the dog in the hotel room tonight. I knew he was a comfort to her, but we didn't need to spend time chasing a canine through a huge cave system.

I tried not to wake Cassidy or Dominic as I entered the hotel room. It had been a long and stressful day and night. As I took my boots off and settled down to get some rest, I noticed Cassidy's sketchbook open. It looked like she was already getting some inspiration.

Who is this figure? It looked like, or it could be...

Best to wait until Cassidy woke up and described it to me. She stirred as I tried to quietly climb into bed. I knew she had a busy day sketching and keeping Dominic entertained. Things were in disarray, clothes scattered here and there, but that was okay. It felt like home.

Time for sleep. The sun would be coming up soon, and I had to meet the team for a late breakfast. We'd get started later today, but that would work just fine. Butch insisted on investigating that crevasse, and everyone wanted to check out Goliath Cave. I thought about calling Mr. Jonas, but it was far too late for that. I may as well wait until I had the full report for him. So far, I could honestly tell him that yes, the caverns were haunted but no one had gotten hurt. Not in any real way.

Right before my eyes closed, I felt my wife's cool hand on my arm. I squeezed her hand and kissed it. Dominic snored between us. We smiled at one another in the dark before we passed out. I didn't dream. I didn't stir, even when my son fussed for breakfast. Eventually, I had to get up. My body was sore; my mind raced ahead of me. *Ugh. Morning so soon.* Hotel coffee was not the best, but it was all we had. And me with no honey for my coffee. Well, sugar would have to do. I depended on coffee far too much, but I wasn't going to abstain today.

"Good morning, beautiful. How did you rest?" I asked Cassidy as she put the baby in his car seat. He loved staring at the musical toy that dangled above him.

"I rested as well as I could without you here. How did last night's investigation go with the team?" Cassidy asked as I handed her a cup of weak coffee.

"We had a few hiccups, but overall, the caves did not disappoint. Joshua and Sierra had a very interesting encounter at the beginning. They saw an apparition almost immediately, a mining car with a dead man inside flew by. There were no rail tracks in the cave and no mention of mining cars in my conversation with Mr. Jonas, but that doesn't mean anything. I mean, naturally at some point there would have been mining cars. Butch and I found a deep hole at the back of Goliath Cave and encountered a shadow person but got no response from it. How was your night?"

"Wow. That sounds incredible!" In a tired voice, Cassidy continued, "It was interesting. Dominic was restless most of the early evening. I don't know whether it was the car ride or the unfamiliar room, but he finally settled down about nine o'clock. I started sketching after that, but it is not finished. The spirit didn't want to cooperate with me."

"Yes, I see you started working on a sketch. What can you tell me about this guy?" I didn't mention that he appeared kind of familiar to me.

Cassidy curled her feet up underneath her. She shook her head and sipped the horrible coffee. "Midas, it is not finished. Like I said, this guy was less than forthcoming. I think he wanted to reveal more but wasn't sure about me. He's very secretive."

I examined her work again. It always amazed me. She was an incredible artist, and she always nailed it. Somehow, her work continued to provide the Gulf Coast Paranormal team with necessary clues.

"Cassidy, this is an exact resemblance to the Cathedral Caverns and to Goliath Cave's entrance. No clues as to who you've drawn on the pathway?" I put the sketch down and went to retrieve Dominic. He must have heard us talking. I needed some morning loving anyway. I loved my son.

"I wish I knew. I'll keep working on that. All I saw was the back of him walking along the paths. He seems to be searching for something. Or maybe someone. I am hoping that as I finish the drawing it will make more sense. I must confess; this wasn't an easy sketch. Not at all."

This was blowing my mind. Was this Mr. Jonas? I fought the urge to call the client and question him. I snuggled with Dominic as Cassidy studied her picture. She closed her eyes and focused inwardly. I managed to keep Dominic happy while she tried to tap into the other realm.

"Nothing. I'll try again later. Ugh. I'm so tired. Would you mind if your son and I hung out here? I don't think I have the energy to get dressed," she said with a sad smile.

I rose from the chair and kissed her. "Of course. Do you want me to take him with me so you can take a nap?"

Cassidy bit her lip thoughtfully. I knew she'd refuse. My wife did not like being away from our son at all. "No, it's fine. You do what you have to do, Midas. I'll be here. Maybe the two of us will nap soon."

I hated that she was so tired. I was told it's a regular thing for new mothers. Cassidy had always been so healthy and energetic. But then again, our son wasn't that old. She put her hands out for the baby, and I gently delivered him to her.

"Can I take this picture to the team? I think it will answer some questions for them; I know it has for me."

"Sure, if you think it will help, but I am not finished. How about taking a picture and leaving that with me?"

"Of course." I snapped a few photos of her sketch and tried to help her tidy up the room.

I knew her visions were accurate, but this one made the hair on the back of my neck stand up. Could it be him? I wanted to get Joshua's take on this since he went chasing after someone last night.

"Do you want me to bring you anything back for breakfast?" I asked as I slid my phone in my pocket.

"Yes. Bring me a sausage biscuit if the biscuits are not hard. If they are, just a sausage patty, please." She grinned mischievously. That was her breakfast weakness, sausage biscuits.

I kissed her one more time. "Got it. I love you."

"I love you too, Midas. Be careful, okay?"

Feeling somewhat rested, I left the room and headed down to the restaurant. Sure enough, most everyone was there, menus at the ready. At least no one scolded me for being late. I sat in the only open chair. I took my phone out of my pocket and put it on the table. Everyone greeted me with some excitement. Like me, they were tired. That I could see.

"Hey, Jericho. Where is Macie? Is she walking Sherman?" I asked as I poured a glass of orange juice from the carafe.

"No. Um, she's in the room. I was telling these guys Macie will not be joining us this morning."

Silence fell over the group, but I kept my game face on. "Alright. Let's review last night's happenings. And there was a lot, I'm sure you'll agree with me. Joshua and Sierra saw the apparition between C and E. Joshua saw a black figure outside the cave and experienced what could be called a time slip at the entrance. Butch and I picked up a shadow object in the light grid, but it would not communicate with us. We had rocks being thrown at us, or they were falling out of midair. And interestingly enough, we found an unmapped cavern. I think we should stick together tonight. Let's work Goliath as a team. What do you guys think?"

Thankfully, the crew seemed excited about that idea. At least we had that going for us. I hoped Macie would come too. I'd have to visit her.

"Cassidy started a sketch last night. With her permission, I am sharing these photos with you. But understand, it is not finished. Joshua, I'd like you to look first. Tell me what you think." I handed him the phone.

Joshua's eyes widened as I placed the phone in his hands. "This is what I saw last night, Midas. No joke. Not the three guys at the entrance but outside in the parking lot. He was in black, but it was this shape. Same shoulders. Same head shape. I think this was the guy."

"Are you sure, Joshua?" Sierra asked as she leaned over his shoulder to examine the photo too.

"Yes. This is exactly what I saw last night when I laid the radio down in the van. When you were trying to reach me. I am sorry about that, by the way. This is what I saw, the back of a man walking along a path. He was always out of reach. I feel like I played chase with him. And that he wanted me to follow him, but I couldn't keep up."

His confession was met with silence. But only for a few minutes. Sierra dug out her mini laptop and began scrolling through her research.

Jericho and Butch talked about the depth of the crevasse and the potential find. After breakfast arrived and we gobbled it down, I reconvened our meeting.

"Okay. Tonight, we stay together. Joshua, I want you to go with Butch into the new cave. Jericho, you'll be on standby. I cannot fit inside, and Butch saw some things that need to be checked out tonight. First, though, I want everyone to go back and get some more rest. There's no need to start so early. Let's meet in the parking lot at three o'clock. How does that sound?"

"More sleep sounds wonderful, Big Brother," Sierra said as she rubbed her husband's back. Joshua was trying to contain his excitement about going into the newly discovered cave.

"Joshua and Jericho, you two check all the radios and monitors before we leave today?"

Jericho laughed and shook his head. "If he'll let me touch anything. Joshua keeps a tight grip on the equipment."

I knew he was joking but also telling the truth as he saw it. Okay, this was a problem. Joshua needed to let go a little if he wanted to shift into other areas of research. And I got the feeling that he did. He couldn't help it. His gifts were starting to emerge. Finally.

"You know, you're right. Challenge accepted. I'll meet you at the van at two." Jericho and Joshua fist-bumped to solidify their deal.

Good. That's settled.

As the group was departing, I stopped Jericho. "I would like to talk to Macie. Do you think she'd be okay with that?"

"I'll text her. I think so, but I'd like to make sure."

I didn't poke him for information. This was between me and Macie. Not anyone else.

"That is fine, Jericho. I need to take a sausage biscuit to Cassidy anyway. I will meet you at your room. Unless she says no. Text me."

Jericho gave me a thumbs-up as he walked away and headed back upstairs to the room he shared with Macie. Supposedly, they were not an item. They had a room with two beds, but they enjoyed one another's company and Jericho loved Sherman almost as much as he loved Macie. Everyone knew how he felt. How she felt was another story.

After dropping off Cassidy's breakfast and promising to return, I made my way to Jericho and Macie's room, contemplating what could be going on with her.

Whatever it was, I was determined to rescue her. I wasn't going to lose another Graves sister.

Never again.

Chapter Ten—Midas

When I got to Jericho and Macie's room, I didn't know what to expect. My stomach was in knots. This was the part of being in charge that strangely enough I enjoyed but also dreaded. Don't ask me to explain it.

I could only guess what Macie was experiencing. Still dealing with the loss of her sister, Jocelyn, no doubt. Why was it so hard to say her name? To even think her name?

Get it together, Midas. It had been a tragic event, caused by an evil entity. It hadn't been Jocelyn's fault. Not even mine. But I had been the guy in charge.

Well, here was the room; I could not delay this any longer. Time to talk to Macie. I only hoped that I could find a way to encourage her. She was not quite like Jocelyn, headstrong and independent, but she was a Graves. I did feel responsible for her well-being, especially if she was going to be a part of this team.

I knocked on the door but didn't have to wait long. "Hello, Jericho. May I come in?"

Jericho flashed his easy smile. He acted as if nothing were wrong at all, but that couldn't be true. "Sure thing. Come in. I'm about to take Sherman out for a walk. He's playful this morning. You guys need anything?" I stepped inside and saw Macie sitting cross-legged on the bed.

"No thank you," both Macie and I answered.

"Great. I'll be back soon," Jericho said as he glanced at Macie. He left us alone, and I closed the door behind him.

"Do you mind if I have a seat?" I pointed to an open chair by the door.

She leaned back on her pillow. She looked out of sorts, like she'd been crying. "Sure thing. Sorry I missed breakfast. You didn't need to come. I just needed a moment."

"Talk to me, Macie. I'm here to listen."

Macie blew a raspberry and sagged back. So like a young person. "I'm fine. I swear."

"I am sure you are, Macie, but you need to talk to me. Or Cassidy. Should I ask her to come instead?" I suddenly felt unsure of myself. Not like me at all.

She stared down at her fingers. "No. That's not necessary. Midas, I am not my sister. I don't know what everyone expects from me. I thought coming to Mobile, being with the team, was what

I needed to do. But now I'm not sure. I don't know what I'm doing here."

Macie glanced up at me as if she were waiting for me to contradict her. I didn't. It wasn't the time to talk. It was the time to listen. I sensed she needed to express herself. And I wanted that for her.

"Jocelyn was driven, determined and independent. God, I always admired her. From day one, I wanted to be like her. She didn't acknowledge fear or accept limits. Jocelyn lived for herself. But I realize I am nothing like her. I'm chasing her shadow."

Macie was right about one thing—she was nothing like Jocelyn. Jocelyn was driven, determined and independent to say the least. She had been all those things. She knew what she wanted and didn't mind leaving others behind to achieve her goals. Just ask Pete Broadus.

"No, Macie, you are nothing like Jocelyn. That's a good thing. Jocelyn's energy was frenetic, where you bring calmness. Jocelyn ran toward danger. You measure the cost and think before you leap. There's nothing wrong with that."

"I am not a seasoned paranormal investigator. I try, but I can't do what she did. I can't snap photos of the dead. I can't see the invisible. I know I'm not my sister...."

I shook my head to dispel her fears. "Macie, no one on this team was seasoned when they became a part of the team. Everyone on this team brings something unique with them, and we do not realize what it is in the beginning. Not until we are put into a stressful situation, unfortunately. Last night when I was calling for Joshua and he would not answer, you and Jericho held your position and let things work out. I am thankful for that. So, let's keep doing that—hold your position. Be an anchor for the team. You will find your purpose, and if it's not with us, that's okay."

Her dark eyes clamped onto mine. "You think so? You really mean that?"

"I wouldn't lie to you, Macie. I want you to be happy." I paused a moment, wondering how to put together my thoughts. "That night, when Jocelyn died, I wanted to die too. That moment, it seemed to go on forever. I couldn't save her, Macie. I am sorry. From the bottom of my heart, I am truly sorry."

Macie climbed off the bed and sat in the chair across from me. "Oh, Midas, I know that. I know you well enough to know you did everything you could. But one day…"

"One day what, Macie?"

She swallowed visibly. "I want to go back to the Leaf Academy. I want to go see where my sister died. I want to see the thing that killed her. And if I can, I want to destroy it." She sobbed once but didn't cry. I didn't know what to say. This was not what I expected from her. Not at all. How should I answer her?

I reached across the table and squeezed her hand briefly. Man, I should have asked Cassidy to come up here with me.

"You don't owe me anything, Midas. I'm asking because I need to do this. I need to go there. Please, help me. Promise me one day we will go back."

Against my better judgment, I looked Macie in the eye and said, "Macie, I promise you. One day, we will go back to the Leaf Academy together."

She rubbed at her eyes with her fingers. "Thank you."

After a minute, I asked, "Are we good? Will I see you this afternoon? We're meeting at the van at three o'clock."

Hopping up from her chair, she said, "Yes. You will see me. Thanks again, Midas. Thanks for hearing me out."

"Anytime, Macie Graves. Remind Jericho that he's supposed to meet Joshua at two o'clock."

91

"Gotcha, Midas, I will be there. And I'll remind Jericho too. You do know we are just friends, right? I mean there is nothing going on."

"You are both grown adults. It's none of my business, Macie."

She frowned at me. "It needs to be. I think people are getting the wrong idea."

"As long as Jericho knows, that's all that matters." I decided that was my cue to leave. "See you guys this afternoon."

Macie was young and had a lot of life to live. A lot to offer the team. I hoped she would stay around long enough to realize that. As far as her relationship with Jericho went, it really wasn't any of my business.

I made my way to my wife and son and decided to call Mr. Jonas to give him an update. After all, he was the one who contacted me and gave the background on the cave. I punched in his number but got nothing. Not a ring or even a voicemail greeting. Maybe it was my signal, since we were out a ways. No matter. I would see him tomorrow because the park would reopen. I would give him my verbal final report then.

Cassidy was changing Dominic when I entered the hotel room. The phone was ringing too. I picked it up but apparently not in time. Whoever was there hung up.

"What is going on with Macie? Did you guys get it sorted out?" Cassidy asked as she kissed Dominic's bare tummy. He grabbed at her long red hair. Such a mischievous child already.

How to answer her question? I didn't dare tell her what I promised Macie. Not today. Not while we were on investigation at the caverns. I know it was wrong keeping a secret from my wife, but I didn't want to think about the Leaf Academy today. Or any other day.

"She's trying to find her place on the team. She is comparing herself to Jocelyn and isn't measuring up in her own mind. I reassured her that she is not her sister and should not compare herself. Macie has her own skills and abilities that she can offer the team, and time will reveal how she best fits in. I hope I helped her."

"I am sure you did, Midas. You are a very good leader. I followed you—that must count for something. This team loves and respects you. Just lead them, Midas."

I kissed her cheek and sat on the bed beside her. "Of course it counts for something. It counts for a lot. Enough talk about the team, Cassidy. Let's talk about me and you."

"Now, Midas, you need to spend time with our son. You have only a few hours before you leave for the cave again. And I need to work on my sketch. There is plenty of time for you and me."

She could read me like a book, but then again, I wasn't the smoothest operator. "You're right, Cassidy. You work on the sketch, and I'll look after Dominic."

I did not know how much my wife and son's presence in my life would ground me. Both of them had stolen my heart. I thought having Cassidy as my wife grounded me, but this little man really changed me forever. I was a father now, and one day he was going to be looking to me for guidance. What a responsibility!

But about tonight...how should I organize things? I knew what I wanted to do—have the whole team in the cave so all of them could stretch their wings and be in on the experience. It would certainly help me to have more eyes and ears down there. With Butch and Joshua going down into the crevasse, I could use some extra hands to get them out in case of an emergency.

That settled it. I would have the whole team in Goliath Cave. Sierra and Macie could monitor the cameras with the iPad and monitor the REM pod and laser grids.

"Midas, stop thinking and rest. Dominic is already asleep. Everything will be okay. You have done this at least a hundred times. You've got everything covered, and the team is ready. Trust them. Trust yourself."

"You're right, Cassidy. I know I'm overthinking everything. Thank you. I think I will close my eyes." I cuddled up to my son and fell fast asleep.

Chapter Eleven—Sierra

It all started in the shower. I'd just applied shampoo to my hair when I heard the voice. A female's voice. She was young, probably a teenager. Then another voice. A young man. The voices were as they always were when I first heard the dead: muffled, as if I were listening to people talk through an apartment wall. I knew what this meant. The spirit world had a message for me. The spirits wanted to talk, and for whatever reason, I was subconsciously opening to them.

I hurriedly finished washing my hair and got out of the shower. Joshua was gone to the nearby home improvement store. No matter how many batteries we packed, there were never enough. I don't know. I kind of think he just wanted a minute to himself. He'd had some intense experiences last night. Way too intense. He didn't get a good night's sleep either.

I needed a moment too. Time to zone out or zone in without interruption. That's what I needed.

Some good old zone-in time.

I could feel myself melting into the moment. Embracing it. This process could not be explained adequately. My grasp on language lacked the refinement necessary to make the curious understand what I meant.

I tidied up the bathroom and got dressed for tonight's investigation, but a comfortable disassociation settled in. Thankfully, I had already called my mother-in-law to check in. As always, those phone calls made me miss home. My mother-in-law was a changed person since her divorce. She was happier, I think. Calmer. My daughter was her life. I was okay with that. I was glad. The more people that loved Emily, the better.

No, I don't want to. Please...let's go...

I sat on the bed and stared out the window. We were on the second floor, and there wasn't much traffic on the walkway. The blue sky and white clouds offered a nice background for staring into nothing, yet seeing everything. I took a deep breath and focused on what I saw, smelled and heard.

*****

White and pink sweater. She wore a sweater, but it wasn't enough to keep her warm. She was cold. Ashley. That was her name—I'd heard that correctly. The teenager never wanted to come here. She liked Tony, but she wasn't sure if she "liked him" liked him. His adventurous spirit excited her, but he didn't have a car. Ashley wanted to date someone who had a car. In fact, she wanted nothing more than to get out of her parents' house. Their constant nitpicking and arguing were driving her mad. Beyond mad.

"Don't be a chicken, Ashley. It's just a hole in the ground. Come down with us. We could be the first people in hundreds of years—or ever—to investigate it."

Ashley shuffled her feet, unsure what to do. She wasn't necessarily scared to go down, but she'd started her period. What if she leaked on her light-colored jeans?

No, she wanted to go home. This wasn't what she signed up for. Bridgette held her hand and shook her head. She needn't have bothered. Ashley had no intention of going down there. Even if Captain Hook hid his stash in that hole. Not that he would. Goliath Cave was far, far away from the ocean.

"We're going home. Come back up here right now. You two are going to break your heads if you aren't careful." Ashley hated the way she sounded. Like a nag. Like her mother. But seriously, she'd at least hoped for a kiss from Tony. Clearly, he wasn't mature enough for her. She heard laughing at the north side of the Goliath near the entrance of the cavern. Why not go hang out with the rest of the teenagers? There were other guys here, weren't there? It's not like she and Tony had an actual date.

Tony grinned at her, showing his gap-toothed smile. Why did she find him cute? Damn it. She sure did. "Ten minutes. Give me ten minutes."

"You've been saying that all night, Tony. I'm going back to the party. This is stupid."

With that, she turned on her heel and headed back to join the rest of the group.

"Hey, Ashley!" Tony whispered furiously. "You can't tell anyone. This is our find, our secret."

Bridgette had already left. She was stomping back up the path. Ashley knew she had a thing for Corey. She definitely had a thing for Corey, and if she was easy enough, he would have a thing for her too. Ashley hoped Bridgette resisted Corey's flirtatious overtures. He was a big fat liar. Unfortunately, Ashley knew that from experience. Even though they hadn't gone all the way. Pretty close, though.

"Fine, it's a secret. Later, Tony. I hope you and Butch have a great time together."

"Hey…" Butch whined after her, but she did not turn around. She was in no mood to argue with either of them. She was cramping like a son of a gun and wanted to go home. Tessa would take her. She was sure of that. Tessa hadn't wanted to come to this stupid party, anyway. Who sneaks into the caverns to party? Spooky-ass place.

For some reason, Ashley turned to look back one more time. Tony didn't notice her longing glance. She sighed as she walked away...

*****

I saw Tony—and Butch! What was going on here? Clearly, they were in the Goliath. Yes, they were in Goliath Cave! How many crevasses were in that place? I wasn't sure what was going on here. I began to get the feeling that Butch wasn't being completely honest with us. Did Midas know?

Ashley hadn't left with Tony after all. Butch said he saw them leave together, but from what I saw, that wasn't true. Was he confused? Did he forget? This wasn't something you'd forget, though, which meant he was likely lying to us. I didn't want to think about that. I paced the hotel room, chewing my fingernail. Yeah, I needed a manicure, but who had time for those?

I needed to see more. I needed to see Butch. How did one tune into a living person? No, I wasn't even going to try that. But Tony... I truly believed Tony wanted his story told. He was the reason why I saw what I saw, at least I believed that.

"Come on, Tony. Talk to me. Show me what you want me to see."

I stopped pacing and peeked out the hotel window. Joshua was in the parking lot with Jericho. The two tech lovers were working out the kinks for tonight's investigation. I glanced at my watch. Okay, forty-five minutes. That was enough time to see something, wasn't it?

I closed my eyes this time. It did no good. None at all. I didn't see a thing. But when I opened them, that was another story.

*****

"Butch, I need five more minutes," Tony whispered to his climbing partner. He couldn't say why he was whispering other than he didn't want anyone to hear. No one besides Butch. It wasn't like anyone was down here. Or had ever been down here. His flashlight wasn't the best, but it worked. The glinting of the flecks of gems in the walls thrilled him. What if those gems were real? His father didn't believe in such things, but why not? Tony believed in the impossible.

He believed there could be a Spanish treasure here. Or if not a Spanish treasure, at least a treasure trove of gems. People occasionally found nice gems here at the Cathedral Caverns. Why not him? Why not Butch?

Tony turned to summon Butch to join him, but he was nowhere to be found. Suddenly, Tony didn't care if anyone heard him. He didn't care if his voice reverberated off the walls around him. He didn't care at all.

"Butch! Come on, man! Where are you? I found something!" He shined his light back on the canteen. It was old and rusted. Could be quite old. Okay, obviously, they weren't the first people down here, but Tony knew the map of this cave from front to back. Not only the Goliath but all of the Cathedral Caverns. This crevasse was not a large cavern but actually a twisting tunnel. But still, it could lead somewhere.

Damn! His flashlight had tanked on him.

"Hey! Butch! Where are you?" He smacked the light, and it came on briefly.

Okay, the exit was two turns to the left.

Left, left and here was the mound. It was dank and slightly moist. Water trickled down the back wall.

But the ladder. The ladder! The rope ladder! It was missing!

Immediately, he began to scream.

"HEY, BUTCH! BUTCH! I'm down here! I'm still down here! Where are you? HEY!"

He screamed and cried at the same time. "BUTCH! THIS ISN'T FUNNY, MAN!" Was Butch playing a trick on him? A joke?

He jumped up, but there was no way he could ever reach the hole above him. He waved his flickering flashlight around, hoping to find something that would help him escape this terrible hole.

SHIT! He was alone down here! What gives? He was just here with Butch! He'd only stepped off the path for a moment. Only a moment!

"ASHLEY! BUTCH!" He screamed their names again and again. He heard voices in the distance, but not for long.

All went quiet. The voices disappeared. The party was over. He was alone in this cave, but for how long?

Then the flashlight went out. He sank down on the ground and cried in the pitch dark. The minutes turned into hours. The hours...maybe into days. He couldn't be sure. He was so hungry. He found water and drank it regularly, but his stomach churned. Churned knowing that his friend had betrayed him. He'd left Tony here.

And he was never coming back...

"Oh, God! Oh, God! Midas!" I picked up the phone to call Big Brother. What was I going to say? I couldn't stop crying. I couldn't stop shaking. I was still shaking uncontrollably when Joshua returned.

Chapter Twelve—Joshua

Why did Midas want me to go down this crevasse with Butch? What was he thinking? I had only climbed the rock wall at the gym, and that was on a dare. I was no cave climber, and Butch was giving me pointers like I knew what the hell I was doing.

Ten minutes of training was not enough. I already knew how to look like a fool on my own; I didn't need anyone's help to do that. I knew I wanted to be more than the tech guy, but this was a bit extreme. Was Midas trying to get me to quit? Was this Sierra's idea? She would have talked to me first unless she and Midas were in this together. Nah, Sierra wouldn't do that. Would she?

Whatever my fears, I was determined to show Midas that I could do this. I was lead investigator material.

"Okay, Joshua. Put on your harness and make sure you tighten it as much as possible," Butch explained, like he was giving instructions to a child. This part I remembered no problem.

Apparently, it wasn't as tight as it needed to be. Butch snatched the belt tighter.

"Ugh! Why does it have to be that tight? I felt the pitch in my voice change."

Butch laughed. "Joshua, if you slip, it will prevent you from snapping your back or sliding out of your harness. Either one of those is bad news. I've seen it happen. It's never good."

"Gotcha, if you say so."

"Trust me, Joshua. I know what I am talking about." You could hear pain of days gone by in Butch's voice. His laughter was long gone. "Snap your d-ring onto the rope and keep pressure at all times. Do not let the rope get tangled around your legs, and take it slow. I am going first. When I get to the bottom, I will signal for you to start your descent. You ready?"

No, I was not ready for this. Who was I kidding? But I could not let him see me sweat. *Pull it together, Joshua, and do not embarrass yourself.* The team gathered around the crevasse to watch us descend. Damn. He made it look easy. My stomach lurched, and I suddenly wanted to pee. Well, too late now.

Butch made it to the bottom, and now it was my turn. Great. Just great.

Sierra kissed my cheek before I began my descent of terror. "Joshua, you can do this. I believe in you. Just be aware of your surroundings at all times."

Midas piped in, "You've got this. Don't forget to switch on your GoPro!"

"Right. Got it."

Here goes nothing. Before I knew it, I was sliding down a rope into the darkness with nothing but a small flashlight to see by. Screaming on the inside, I practically landed on the floor. I suddenly wanted to go back and watch the monitors.

You wanted this Joshua, so suck it up and do this.

"You did great, Joshua, like an old pro," Butch said. That was a crock, but I thanked him for his kind comment.

When I gathered my bearings, I reached for my radio. "Midas, come in; this is Joshua. Radio check."

"I hear you loud and clear, Joshua."

I began waving my flashlight around. Such a big room. You would never know it looking through the crevasse. So much to see in here. Everywhere I shined my light, I caught small reflections of something in the rocks. The air was thick in here with the sounds of dripping water in the distance. It seemed to echo off the walls and ceiling. The darkness was like nothing I had ever seen or experienced. The light seemed to pierce the darkness like a knife through butter.

"Okay, Butch, where do we start?"

"Let's see what is causing the light reflections first."

"You lead the way, and I will follow you."

We made our way through rocks protruding through the floor, uneven walking areas, and cracks through rocks, when we finally reached a wall loaded with gem reflections. Yes, they were in the stones embedded in the wall. All kinds of gemstones.

Could this be what those young people were after when Tony went missing? Could this be what the creepy miner guy that Sierra and I saw was protecting?

"Joshua, let's go. We should make our way to the dripping water. Do you hear it? We need to see if it is fresh water just in case we need it." Butch reached for his bag and began walking toward the sound. "It's not far."

"Just in case we need it? I filled my water bottle before I left the van. I don't plan on drinking this stuff."

Had Butch been in this cave before? He was acting like he had, and not just for a short excursion. Why would we want to find water? It wasn't like we were going to spend the night in here or something. I knew where the rope was located, and I planned on heading back to it sooner rather than later. Between Midas and Jericho, they could pull me out. But this was no time to question him.

"Okay. Butch, I am following you."

Out of nowhere, a small rock hit me in the back. It fell to the ground, making a thud as it bounced off into the darkness. It was not a hard hit but certainly like someone trying to get my attention. Like Sierra did when she didn't want to call my name anymore.

What was that, and was it a warning? Or just a rock falling? I mean, we were in a cave, after all. But then it happened again. This time, it hit the back of my calf, and it stung like fire. That was no mere falling rock. Someone had flung that sucker.

"Stop, Butch! I got hit. Someone threw a rock at me!"

"No way. There's no one down here but us. Are you sure?"

Butch's disbelief pissed me off, but I didn't have time to argue with him.

More rocks began to fall around us, like someone was trying to get our attention. Or the roof was caving in.

My radio crackled once. I tapped on my walkie, but there was nothing but static. "Too much interference," Butch said sadly. "I was afraid of that."

We began to make our way to the sound of the water, my senses already heightened because of the falling rocks. Everything seemed to catch my attention. Butch knew where to place his feet as we made our way through the uneven terrain.

Hmm... I know he is a professional, but this feels wrong.

Everything felt like he had been here before and was looking for something specific. What could it be? Well, only time would tell what was going on. I just hoped it wouldn't put anybody in danger.

The sound of the water was getting closer as we made our way deeper into the darkness. Yes, I could smell the water, and the air was beginning to change as we drew closer to it. It didn't smell fresh or drinkable. More like foul and nasty. I don't know whether it was the humidity from the water or something else down here with us.

I only knew that I didn't like this feeling. I hoped we wrapped this up soon. Just then, the radio broke the silence in the air. Midas was calling. Thank God! Was it finally working again?

"Joshua? Come in. This is Midas."

I couldn't grab the walkie fast enough. Butch remained about ten steps ahead of me. "I hear you, Midas."

"Your GoPro isn't picking up much. Do you have it on night vision?"

I tapped on it to be sure. "Yes, it's on night vision." I smacked the helmet a few times. "How's that?"

"Great. Works better now. Have you found anything yet? Any signs? Any encounters?"

Butch had stopped and was waiting for me. What should I say? *I think this guy isn't on the up-and-up?* I liked Butch, but something was wrong here. "Nothing yet. We are making our way to the sound of water. I will radio you when we get there. Joshua out."

"Roger that. Midas out."

Just as I finished talking to Midas, we continued our journey. Butch waved me forward, and I reluctantly followed him. The light from the flashlights reflected off the pool of water and brightened the area around us.

Butch's strange behavior seemed to have increased—it was as if he had to find something. He invited me to taste the water, but I refused. We then began to look around this section of the cave. We were looking for anything that could be causing the paranormal activity we experienced yesterday.

I saw nothing. Nothing but fragments of gemstones, rocks and more rocks, and darkness.

The kind of darkness you could get lost in.

We rested for a bit since it took a lot out of us to navigate the terrain down here. Butch was quiet, which wasn't completely out of character for him. What did he expect to find down here?

"Butch, are you okay? Maybe we should do an EVP session down here. What do you think?"

"Yes, Joshua, I am okay. I am just trying to keep us safe. Yeah, let's do it."

Before I even removed the digital recorder, I heard a voice. A whisper at first. Then louder.

Butch...

Was that the sound of Midas calling down the crevasse? We had a radio, and I had already talked to him a little bit ago. All Midas had to do was call me.

Shining a light briefly in Butch's direction, I could see that he heard it too. Maybe even knew the voice. I had the creepy-crawlies, that odd sick feeling that hit me when high strangeness occurred.

Out of the darkness, I heard the whisper again. *BUTCH!*

I fumbled around for the radio to call Midas, but the voice returned a third time.

What are you doing here, Butch?

Butch appeared to be frozen in place, unsure what to do. I called Midas, and there was nothing but static. This was not my fault. These walkie-talkies had a limit. I knew they were working. Jericho and I had charged them and checked them out.

I turned my attention back to the voice we were hearing. Quiet was all we were getting now. Then Butch screamed out, "Tony, is that you?"

Why was he calling for Tony? Butch had flipped out on me, and I had to get us out of this cavern. Butch trembled next to me. He didn't cry, but he certainly looked close to tears.

After a few minutes of silence, I convinced him to get moving so we could wrap up this investigation. We began moving around the perimeter to get back to the rope to get out. The pace wasn't as deliberate as before, but we were moving. That's what I wanted.

But then, there it was again, that young voice.

Butch...why?

This was getting to be too much. I tried to radio Midas again and heard nothing but static.

Static! I didn't need static! I needed to talk to Midas. He should know about this voice and how personal it was getting.

Out of the darkness again, the voice yelled, *BUTCH, I KNOW YOU ARE HERE!*

It wasn't soft anymore. It was angry and insistent.

Butch screamed back. "What do you want, Tony?"

Why was Butch communicating with him? Did they have some kind of history? I wished I knew more about Tony. I needed to get us back to the opening now. Not later!

"Butch, pull yourself together. We have to get moving. We are almost there!"

He shook himself visibly. His square jaw popped in determination. "Roger that, Joshua."

I could hear the shakiness in his voice. Then, out of the darkness, we stumbled on worn clothing that appeared to be old and fragile. What was it doing down here?

This wasn't good. This wasn't good at all.

The clothing might be old but not as old as the clothing the skeletal miner had been wearing. No, not that old. This was more recent. Oh, and the smell. I caught a whiff of it before I saw it. Death was near. It had its own smell. I knew it well.

Ah, and there it was. I shined my flashlight on the ground. I gagged a little as I spotted the white bones. It was a skeleton! A skeleton with a canteen lying next to its right hand.

Butch turned white as a sheet. He sank to his knees as if every bit of life had left him. He screamed out, and it echoed through the stale chamber. "Tony! I didn't know. I thought you already left! I didn't see you! I called you, and you didn't answer. Man! Tony! Oh, God!" He was in full-on sob mode, and I was stuck down here with him and the skeleton.

Now I was freaked out. I needed to call Midas. "Midas, this is Joshua. Come in! Come in! Midas, come in!"

Nothing but static. Static!

BUTCH...

At this point, I was past ready to get out of this cave. If Midas would only answer the damn radio, I would know that I was still connected to the outside world. Right now, I felt like I was all alone with a flipped-out Butch and a voice in the darkness.

"Okay, Butch, let's get to the opening so I can radio Midas and we can get out of here. Get your ass up, or I am going to drag you out of here. Now!"

He didn't argue but climbed to his feet wiping his eyes. He stumbled beside me.

Eventually, we made our way to the opening, and once again I radioed Midas.

"Midas, this is Joshua. Come in. We've got to come up! Butch is coming up first."

"Is he injured?"

I sighed as I helped Butch get hooked up. "I'll explain when we get topside. Come on, Midas! Help us!"

Thankfully, the questioning ended and ten minutes later I was topside. I would never go down there again.

Chapter Thirteen—Cassidy

Baby Dom was especially sleepy today. Little babies slept a lot, I'd learned. Now, if I'd just let him sleep without harassing him, that would be great. Still, these long stretches of sleep worried me.

I checked him repeatedly to make sure he was breathing fine. That he didn't have a fever—he was a sweaty little thing—but he was always fine. Nothing wrong with my son at all. Just a drowsy baby with a need to sleep. Constantly.

Sierra told me repeatedly that I should count myself lucky that Dominic enjoyed napping. She also said that these days wouldn't last, but I still worried over him. I even asked the pediatrician about it. He too said I was concerned over nothing. It worried me when my son preferred to sleep rather than play with his Mommy and Daddy.

But I wasn't one to look a gift horse in the mouth. If Dominic needed to sleep, then so be it. I could resist temptation. At least now while I had work to do. Yes, I liked snuggling with my son, but if he needed his sleep, I would just have to resist.

Midas left about an hour ago. We spent time holding the baby, holding one another, whispering promises to each other about our future. I believed him. I'd never thought much about the idea of soulmates, but now that I'd met Midas, I thought a lot about it. Midas had to be my soulmate, right? We were tied together in more ways than one. It was too fantastic to believe that we'd met by complete accident.

With just Dominic and me in the hotel room, I picked up the sketchbook and held my pencil at the ready. Of course, now that I set my mind to work, Dominic woke up occasionally. Luckily, he only stared at me, poked out his tongue to indicate he was hungry, and then fell fast asleep again. I guess he wasn't that hungry. I took everything within me not to kiss him, to hold him. To pick him up.

Cassidy Demopolis, focus! The team might need your help.

Just as well. I needed to sketch. I needed to finish my work. There was a story that had not been fully realized, and it affected Midas. I was sure of that. I stared at the unfinished sketch. "Okay. It's time to show the whole truth. Tell me, show me what happened to you. Please, let us help you."

I was back on the path. Inside the cavern. It was dark but not so dark that I couldn't recognize my surroundings. Strange. I'd never been to the Cathedral Caverns or the infamous Goliath Cave, but I knew it. Just as well as I knew my own home.

The breathtaking height, the tiered walkways, the strange formations, they used to frighten me when I first arrived here, when I first began my duties, but not anymore. I wasn't afraid anymore. In fact, it was my second home.

Or it had been. Before I lost my son.

And then the vision blurred. Or perhaps it was the man's eyes that blurred. Yes, I could sense his deep sadness as I began a new sketch. This one would be different than the other one. There was more than one person in this sketch. But who were they?

I whispered to whoever might be listening, "Tell me. Tell me what you want me to see."

And I did see.

I saw the same man, this time in profile. An ordinary face, lined by worry and years of work. Despite his age, he had broad shoulders and a steady walk, not a halting step. He was strong. Strong and steady. In fact, when he was younger, his wife liked to call him the Rock. Not that he was her rock anymore.

He had failed her in every way. But he still had a chance to make it right. Make it right before the cancer killed him. Loretta didn't even know about it. She had enough to worry her heavy heart. Enough grief. Leeland Jonas' death couldn't be prevented, not according to the doctor, but he could do this.

"Oh my God! This is Mr. Jonas!" I couldn't believe this. What did this mean? I shook the thought away and kept sketching as he spoke and invited me to see. To see him in his last days.

I had to find Tony. No matter what it cost. I had no time for long treatments and medications. He had promised Loretta so long ago that he would bring Tony home.

Oh, so many broken promises. He never kept that promise. But as long as he had breath in his body....

Tonight, he was alone. Walking, searching, moving around the complicated, unknowable layout of the Cathedral Caverns. Every turn he made, he knew. Every step he climbed, he had climbed a hundred times before, but he was going to do it again. And again. As long as he could.

He had to find what he lost. The greatest treasure of his life had been his son.

"He had lost someone he loved deeply. His son. He'd lost his son!" I whispered as I paused my sketching. Feeling his loss, tears came to my eyes, but I had no time to cry. Leeland Jonas was pouring out his heart.

The boy had been gone quite some time, but even after all these years, he could not quit. He had to find him. He had promised the boy's mother; he had promised himself. Why couldn't he keep his promise? Ashley confessed that many of the teens had been there that night. Many of them hanging out, drinking and smoking, but not Tony. Not Butch. They had dreams of finding treasure. How many times had he told that boy there was no treasure here! Anything that had been here had been removed long ago. Long, long ago.

But Leeland Jonas would not quit. He would keep his promise!

Tony! Where are you, son?

No, Tony was not his true son. They were not blood-related, but he had been the son that Leeland Jonas had always dreamed of.

Bright. Brave and lucky. So bright. He would have no problem getting into those highfalutin schools. Smart like his mother, Loretta. Now, that was a smart woman. Tony was brave, and he was not afraid of a challenge. Even tough challenges excited him, and Tony always met them. Attendance awards. Straight A's. Every challenge presented to him.

But Tony was gone. He was gone, and Loretta continued to weep night and day. Leeland was supposed to protect everyone who entered there, even the teenagers who broke the rules and showed up to party.

Yes, he loved Tony with all his heart.

Something told him that he was here. Somewhere in this cavern system. So he walked one more time. One more night. Leeland Jonas knew how obsessed Tony had been with the caverns. He tried to discourage him, but Tony would not listen to anything he had to say. Like most teenage boys, Tony thought he knew everything.

About everything.

The vision ended abruptly. Disappointed by the loss of contact, I continued, scratching and erasing the images like a wild woman. Mr. Jonas, his face stricken with sadness. The first signs of the disease that would eventually kill him unseen but his spirit broken.

I wept as I drew him.

But then I saw someone else. A boy. No, make that a teenager. He wasn't alive. He wasn't as solid as Leeland Jonas, but he was there nonetheless. He knew Mr. Jonas looked for him. He knew, but he couldn't reach him. Not yet.

He would, though. We would make sure of that. I wiped tears from my eyes with the back of my hand. And then I continued to sketch. The blackness grew around the figures, and the darkness of the cave threatened to hide them forever.

But it wouldn't.

Somehow I knew, with Midas and the team's help, they would emerge into the light.

Chapter Fourteen—Midas

Something was wrong, very wrong. I couldn't help but think of Sierra's phone call. What she'd seen, Butch and Tony together, I didn't know what to make of it. Was she seeing correctly? She was convinced that she was, and I had no reason to doubt her, but she insisted that we keep it from the rest of the team. We needed evidence to prove or disprove her vision. As always, Sierra liked to play by the book.

Obviously, the occurrences that happened below Goliath Cave had brought things to a head.

Joshua was in commando mode, and Butch was quiet and solemn. What happened down there? I wanted to know, but Joshua was determined to keep his thoughts to himself for the moment. Butch appeared shaken. Jericho made sure they were hydrated and not physically hurt. He gave them the all-clear, and I waited impatiently to know what exactly happened. The GoPro footage had been sketchy at best. Breaking in and out, showing static much of the time. I was at a loss and more than a little concerned.

Butch was still not talking. He was still sitting there with a look of guilt and sorrow. I could tell Joshua needed a minute to gather himself before he filled me in on the details. Sierra quickly ran over to Joshua to comfort him and get him settled. He was quite rattled by whatever happened down there. Sierra calmed him down, and then he was ready to share. Butch, on the other hand, appeared to be in shock.

This troubled me no end.

Finally, the younger man asked, "Midas, did you hear us when I called you? I mean before we returned to the opening?" His voice sounded frustrated with a touch of anger.

"No, Joshua. I did not. The radio has been here with me the whole time. We've all been waiting to hear from you."

He sighed and glanced at Butch. "We heard a voice," Joshua blurted out. He was breathing like a man who had just run a marathon.

"Did I hear you right, Joshua? You heard a voice?" I was immediately intrigued.

Josh nodded and then glared at Butch, who still wasn't saying anything at all. "Yes, we did, and it was communicating with Butch. I think it was the missing kid. Tony."

"Tell me, what did the voice say?"

Joshua was still out of breath and speaking between deep gasps of air. Whatever or whoever they encountered had greatly affected both men. Could that be the key to the mystery we were trying to solve? I wanted to know more, but I needed to let Joshua have some time to gather himself.

We turned to other things, like reviewing the GoPro footage and checking other camera footage. Sierra suggested that we do some EVP sessions to gather more information.

"Here, Big Brother. You get us started," she said as she handed me a digital recorder.

I accepted the equipment and checked the volume. "My name is Midas. We are not here to hurt you or scare you. My friends and I are here to help you. Will you tell me your name?"

I heard nothing but the natural sounds of the caves. Rocks crumbling. Water dripping. Echoes of bats flying above us.

Then out of the quiet, we heard a single disembodied voice.

Butch!

Okay, that surprised me, but I kept it together. "Is that your name or are you wanting to talk to Butch?"

Quietness returned to the caves as we waited for a response. Who was wanting to talk to Butch and why? Hopefully, Joshua could give me more information when he calmed down.

Again, I heard the voice.

Butch!

Each time the voice spoke, Butch appeared to sink a little more.

Butch, why?

I wished Butch would speak up. It was obvious that the spirit wanted to talk to him. He needed to come clean. It would be good for his soul, and for all of us.

Then, Joshua blurted out, "It is Tony, Midas. It is Tony. Sierra was right about what she saw." Joshua stood to his feet and shed his harness. He was clearly getting angrier by the minute. "Midas, it's true. Tony and Butch discovered this crevasse years ago. Together. Butch was with Tony when he went missing."

My heart skipped a beat, and I felt sick. Everything was beginning to make sense now. Sierra had nailed it and Joshua witnessed it. Yes, it all made sense. Butch's determination to get down in the crevasse and explore—his knowledge of this cave was more than that of a recreational exploration by an experienced caver.

Why was he holding back? What was happening with Butch? What had he done?

"Midas, we found skeletal remains down there. I believe they must belong to Tony." Joshua had regained his composure and was now spilling the beans on Butch.

"Butch and Tony explored this cave together years ago when Tony went missing. Butch left the cave and pulled up the rope ladder, leaving Tony down there to die," Joshua spat angrily.

Butch cried out through his tears, "It was an accident, Joshua. I looked for Tony. I swear I did!"

Butch...why?

"Okay, Butch, it is time to come clean with your knowledge of what happened here and your involvement. I have the safety of this team to think about. Right now, you are a part of the team. Start talking."

Butch shook his head and wiped his eyes. "Alright, Midas. Tony and I, when we were teenagers, came here to party with a group of our friends. At that time, I was just beginning to do caving and climbing. I did not know Tony that well; we just met at the party and decided to explore the cave. We found this crevasse and decided to check it out."

Drinking the last of his bottle of water, Butch paused for a moment. He finally met my gaze and continued, "We got separated after we entered the crevasse. I was intrigued with our find. Gemstones were everywhere. It was like a lost world. I guess I lost track of time. I honestly thought Tony left with Ashley. It was clear she wanted to be with him. They were having an argument before we went down, so I assumed he climbed out and left with her. I did not see his light or hear his voice when I called for him. I left the cave and pulled up the ladder. It was an accident, Midas, just an accident by a teenager."

I knew Butch didn't believe that. I could hear it in his voice, see it in his face. Fine. I was glad he got that off his chest, but that was no excuse. No excuse for withholding necessary information from us. All these years, Butch had an idea where Tony might be, and he never went back to find him.

How could he live with himself? How was it that Mr. Jonas contacted me, of all people? Did he know that Butch was on the Gulf Coast Paranormal team? This was strange. Far too strange.

"Jericho and Macie, take Sherman and Butch out of the cave. Please go back to the van. Joshua, Sierra and I will take care of the equipment and handle things in here."

Macie nodded sadly, and Jericho put his hand on her shoulder. She did not push it away. Both appeared disappointed. They were probably disappointed in Butch, like I was.

But Butch wasn't having any of it. "No, Midas, I have to see this through. It was my fault, and I must make it right. I should have told you, I know, but I had to come back. I had to find him." He was yelling at me now.

I growled back at him, "You are now a liability to the team, Butch. You need to leave the cave."

Butch's jaw popped and his fists were clenched, but after a few seconds of staring at me, he agreed. "Fine. I will leave. I am sorry you think I am a liability. I wanted to help Tony."

Butch gathered the climbing gear to take back to the vehicle. Joshua appeared relieved to say goodbye to the harness. Sierra and I began discussing our plan to deal with the spirit of Tony. Sure enough, the GoPro footage from Joshua's helmet cam revealed the skeletal remains on the floor of the cave. The position of the skeleton was one of someone who sat down and gave in to death's grip. If it was indeed Tony, it was a pitiful image. Here had been someone so young with his whole life ahead of him. It was obvious that Tony wanted to be found, but why now? Now, with Butch gone, we needed to help him, if possible.

We decided to put the digital recorder away. Tony was pretty powerful to be heard as a disembodied voice. "Tony, this is Midas. I brought Butch here. He wanted to find you."

Butch...

"Butch is not here anymore. I sent him out. But I can help you. My friends can help you too."

Again, the voice echoed Butch's name off the walls. How was I going to get Tony to talk to me? Like he was reading my mind, Joshua handed me a rusty old canteen.

"Midas, use this as a trigger object. We found it next to the skeletal remains. It may have belonged to Tony."

"Perfect, Joshua." I accepted the item, and together the three of us sat down not too far from the crevasse. "We've got to call the authorities and get them here."

Sierra looked saddened. "I'd like to continue to try and help Tony before we call the police. We have found his body, but his soul is trapped. I don't know why. He thinks he is trapped, Midas."

I agreed with her and decided to continue our attempts at communication. "Tony, I have your canteen."

I could hear nothing, but Sierra's eyes widened. "I can hear him, Midas. He says he needs water. Can you fill the canteen for him? He is in pain." Sierra clutched her stomach as if she were feeling his pain.

"Yes, I can do that for you, Tony. I have water." Joshua poured water into the canteen, and we placed the rusty container on the floor of the cave, right between us.

To my surprise, it wasn't Sierra who spoke up first but Joshua. "He says he's hungry too. So hungry."

Now, we are communicating. I looked at Joshua and noticed that he was doubled over in pain. What was happening to my friend? Was he experiencing the pain that Tony was experiencing? Could it be that Joshua was also a physical medium, or was he just connected to Tony because of his close contact with his remains?

"Joshua, are you okay?"

"I don't know, Midas. I think I need to leave this cave. Can you take me out of here?"

I believed that Joshua needed to get out of this cave, but leaving Sierra here to deal with Tony by herself would be wrong. That would go against everything inside of me. I wanted to finish helping Tony, and he was talking to us now. I couldn't be sure he would be willing to talk to us later. I must finish this tonight.

Sierra helped Joshua gather his things. "Midas, I will stay down here and finish the investigation and help Tony."

"Sierra, I don't like this," Joshua complained, still clutching his stomach.

"It will be okay. Take the iPad and watch me on the camera. You need to get out, Joshua. I can handle this. You two need to listen to me. For real. Big Brother, I will be okay. I'm not going to take any risks. I promise. I'm sure as heck not going down there." Sierra pointed toward the hole in the floor.

Joshua was ready to fight about it, but he was doubled over at this point. I had no choice but to do as Sierra asked. "Fine, but I'm coming right back."

I made my way out of the cave with Joshua, trying to carry him as much as he would allow me. Navigating the terrain alone was one thing, but with two people and one of them sick, it was a challenge. We finally made it to the entrance of the Cathedral Caverns and headed toward the van. Joshua began to perk up when we exited the cave.

"Midas, I can make it to the van. I'm feeling better. At least I can stand. Please go check on my wife. You know how stubborn she is. Get back to Sierra. Please."

"Are you sure you can make it to the van?" Macie and Jericho were making their way toward us now. I didn't see Butch at all.

"Yes, I can do this. Go!"

I did not want to leave him, but I needed to get back to Sierra. I handed Joshua off to Macie and caught Butch's eye. He was sitting in the van staring at us.

Butch, what am I going to do with you?

I'd have to solve that problem later.

I ran back inside as fast as I could.

Chapter Fifteen—Sierra

Confusion. That's what I experienced. I swallowed, but it was hard to swallow. Oh, this wasn't me. This was Tony!

What day is it? How long have I been here? One day? Two days? A week. I could no longer cry. I was too hungry and tired to continue to explore in the darkness. One false step, and I would fall even further into the black. Surely, Butch would come back for me.

But no one ever came. Once I heard a voice. Not a familiar voice but certainly someone talking. Who would be down here in the crevasse? Who? A search party?

In response, I screamed for help. I screamed for all I was worth. But the voice faded as whoever it was moved away from me. Had they been above me?

"Come back! Please, come back! Dad! I'm sorry!"

I couldn't manage to do anything else. I collapsed beneath the opening and stared up into the blackness.

I prayed, but nothing happened. Nobody came for me. Nobody...

"Tony, I am here for you. I came for you. I can show you how to get out."

I hear you, but I can't see you. Are you real?

I could smell him. He smelled so bad. He smelled like death. Only it didn't turn me off. It didn't make me want to run. Instead, it made me want to throw myself into this session. Tony had to leave here. The poor teenager was trapped in a pit of his own making. He didn't know he was dead. He didn't realize he could leave. I had to help him understand.

Oh, this was going to be heartbreaking.

"Yes, I'm real, Tony. I'm a searcher. We've been looking for you for a long time. I need you to come out of there," I said with as much confidence as I could muster.

He didn't say anything at first. Yes, I felt his confusion. He was so confused.

I'm not supposed to be here. I don't want Dad to find out. I broke the rules.

Then I saw him clearly. He'd been a handsome young man. Not too tall but not too short. He had short brown hair and stubble on his chin. He wasn't a skeleton now but a living teenager. He was showing me who he really was. I waved at him, and to my surprise, he waved back.

"Your dad isn't mad at you, Tony. He just wants you to come home. Are you ready to go home? I can lead you out."

But the crevasse...I don't have a ladder. No ropes. Nothing. I'm stuck here. Forever.

Oh, the horrible sadness inside him. Hopelessness. It was terrible and destructive. It had kept him imprisoned here. How was I going to lead him out?

I heard footsteps walking toward me. Midas had returned, but I held up my hand to keep him back. This was a difficult situation already. I didn't want Tony to be even more confused. Midas nodded but squatted down near the entrance and waited. Suddenly, I had an idea. I picked up my flashlight and walked toward the crevasse.

"Careful, Sierra," Midas whispered, but I ignored him. I needed him to keep quiet.

Tony's spirit wavered in and out now. I could feel him one second but then sensed that he was ready to flee the next. I had to move fast.

"Tony, I'm going to shine this light for you. When you see the light, I want you to move toward it. Okay?" Again, I sensed him fading. He was not strong and not completely in his right mind. He wanted to leave, but he didn't know how.

I can't leave. I don't know how to climb. Butch left me...

"I know, Tony. Don't worry about Butch. I will help you. I need you to trust me. If you focus on the light, you can leave. Do you see it?" I turned on the light and waved the flashlight, hoping the ghost would see it.

I see it. But I can't climb.

"You don't need to climb, Tony. Just watch the light and move toward it. That's all you have to do. Please, trust me."

I will try. I think I see it. Oh, it's so bright. Are you an angel?

I couldn't help but smile inwardly. How could anyone think I was an angel?

"Follow the light, Tony. Pay no attention to anything else. Only the light. Are you coming up?"

I could sense that he wanted to trust me. Wanted to believe me. I pounced on that. "What do you have to lose, Tony? I can help you, but you need to do this. Move toward this light. Just beyond this light is another light. It's even brighter. If you go to that second light, you'll be able to go home. Please, Tony. Try!"

Time was running out. I couldn't explain it, but I knew it for a fact. These opportunities didn't come around often. God would open the door for only a few seconds. Tony needed to move while the opportunity was available to him. Yes, we were here for a reason, and that was Tony.

Suddenly, Tony's spirit whooshed out of the crevasse with surprising strength, practically knocking my flashlight out of my hand. He said nothing, but his joy was palpable.

I rolled over on my back to catch my breath. Above me, with my mind's eye, I could see the light of heaven. It was open to Tony! He swirled around, bouncing between me and the light above.

"No, Tony! Go! Don't stay here! Go home!"

And he did.

Exhausted and saddened by the experience, I cried. Big Brother joined me, but he didn't make me leave or force me to get up. He sat beside me and let me cry it out. Moving people was always both a joy and a huge sadness. Just knowing people's souls were trapped on this earth....

At least there was one less now.

Yes, one less.

Eventually, Midas and I left the cave to catch our breath before returning to remove all of our equipment.

Jericho locked the gate, and we left the Cathedral Caverns forever. I would never come back here again. Never.

I leaned on Joshua's shoulder and found my strength. Even though we had traveled a long way, being with Joshua felt like home.

And that's where I wanted to be.

Chapter Sixteen—Midas

Mystery solved as to what was haunting Goliath Cave. Tony's spirit wanted to get out of the cave and find peace. Thankfully, we were able to do that. Or at least Sierra was able to do that.

I was sure the old skeleton miner in the cart was trying to lead us to help Tony get rescued. There were no reports of a ghostly miner from Mr. Jonas or anywhere on the Internet. Mr. Jonas didn't seem like the sort of man who would leave out important information like that.

The family could have closure knowing that Tony had been found. Time to call Mr. Jonas.

I called the phone number, but nothing happened. What was going on? This was a new phone, and I shouldn't have any problems.

Well, I would drive out there and meet him at the park. I had to meet the police there and show them the location of the skeletal remains anyway. I arrived at the park, and I was greeted by a young woman with "Docent" on her name tag.

"Hello, I'm Midas from Gulf Coast Paranormal. I am looking for Mr. Jonas."

She replied with an obviously bewildered look, "There is no Mr. Jonas working here anymore. Are you sure you have the right name?"

I couldn't process what she was saying. "I just met him here in the parking lot three days ago. He contacted me about a haunting in Goliath Cave. I have the email here on my phone. Let me show you."

I pulled out my phone and opened my email. But there was no message from Mr. Jonas. What the hell? *Okay, now I am losing it.*

I tried to explain myself to the docent, but I was getting nowhere fast. "I swear Mr. Jonas asked me to come. He said there was a haunting in the cave. Look, here is the key to the gate." I dropped them in her hand.

I resorted to telling her what I knew about Tony and explaining the paranormal activity we found in the cave. As I was trying to convince her I wasn't crazy, the police and the medical examiner pulled up to remove the skeletal remains.

As if someone shocked her with electricity, the docent was reminded of an article pinned to the bulletin board in the office. "I think I know what case you are referring to. Please wait here."

After she left, I explained to the police where the remains were located so they could retrieve them. Strangely enough, they didn't question me about how I found the body. It was as if they knew they would find something here one day.

The police began their work, and the docent returned with the faded article of a young man who was reported missing.

The name of the father was mentioned in the article too. It was Leeland Jonas, and his son's name was Tony.

Holy crap!

Could this be the same people we were dealing with in this investigation? I was still reading the article when she presented me with an obituary of Mr. Leeland Jonas.

It couldn't be! I had just talked to this man and walked with him in this park.

I looked at the date on the obituary, and it was published last year. Mr. Jonas said he wanted someone else to know about the events happening here and that he would be leaving soon.

Could it be that our reputation was known by the wandering spirits of the dead?

Could it be that he knew we would find his son?

No matter, it was finished, and it was time to leave this case with the authorities. As far as they knew, we were just amateur cave climbers who stumbled upon a body.

I made my apologies to the docent for any inconvenience. She was kind with her words and thanked me for our care of the facilities, but neither one of us could explain it.

Time to return to my family. Maybe Cassidy would have the sketch completed—that is, if Dominic was cooperative this morning. I think he was ready to go home too. The drive to the hotel wasn't long but long enough to give me time to think about all that had happened.

Was our most recent client a ghost? How would I explain that to the team?

Entering the hotel room, I found my wife staring at her sketch. Her face was a mixture of emotions, none of which I could read.

"What is it, Cassidy?"

"You have to see for yourself, Midas."

I accepted the sketch and quickly studied it.

It couldn't be, but there he was—Mr. Jonas and a young man walking away. That had to be Tony!

Relief swept over me as I fell onto the bed beside Cassidy. I began telling her everything the docent told me and about the articles that I saw.

"Midas, it all makes sense now! Why this case tugged at you so hard...this was the case that pulled you back. Mr. Jonas knew the love and connection you have with our son. He knew you would understand that the bond is strong even in death, and he needed you to help him find his son so he could be at rest with him."

I could no longer hold back the tears and emotions that I was feeling. I was in the safest place possible with my wife beside me. She kissed me, and I kissed her back. And as if she had known me all my life, Cassidy changed my focus from myself to the team.

"How is the team, Midas?"

The team. What was I going to do about the team? Everyone performed excellently, especially Joshua, who stepped up his game. The only weak link was Butch. What was I going to do about him? He withheld information that could have put the team in jeopardy. It was definitely something I would have to deal with in the coming days.

But not today.

"I sent them back to Mobile. There was no need for them to stay here. I can finish here. They were pretty rattled from the past couple days."

"What do you need me to do, Midas?" Cassidy said as she leaned closer. Her skin smelled soft and pretty, like soap and honey.

"Let's get packed up and head home. The authorities said they would contact me when they officially identified the remains. And they would let me know when they are going to bury them. I want to be there, especially if they belong to Tony."

After stuffing our chaos back into two suitcases and the baby's diaper bag, we made our way home. We were exhausted but relieved that we successfully completed another case. And as intense as this one was, it felt good to be back. Cassidy and Dominic took naps while I drove, which gave me plenty of time to think about what to do about Butch.

*****

It had been about a month since we were at the Cathedral Caverns, and here I was, driving back. The authorities finally confirmed that the poor boy Butch and Joshua found inside the crevasse was Tony Jonas. Today was the day they were laying him to rest beside his father. Something was tugging at me again. Cassidy and Dominic, as always, slept in the car. Which I was glad for. Maybe Dominic would not be restless when we got to the cemetery.

We arrived after the service, which was fine by me. No one would have known me anyway. And I was here for Mr. Jonas and Tony.

We walked to the graveside, and lo and behold, there was Mr. Jonas' grave. Sturdy, weed-free grass covered it, proving that he'd been at rest for a while. Or had he?

Tony's fresh grave was beside him. Finally, after so many years, Mr. Jonas could be at peace with his son. I deposited the flowers I brought and knelt between the graves to offer my respects.

Dominic began to get fussy. Cassidy took him back to the truck to settle him down.

I reflected on the events that led up to the investigation and the investigation itself. So much had happened with the team. All the mysterious events, the ups and downs, were mind-blowing.

Well, it was time to get the family to the room for the night, as we were driving back tomorrow to prepare for the next case. Our work here was done at last.

I gazed toward the west to see the sun setting, and as I did, I saw a figure standing in front of me.

He was a good twenty feet away, but I recognized him. Mr. Jonas! His smiling face beamed as he reached out his hand. Tony appeared with him. There they were, father and son, hand in hand.

He just smiled and waved at me. I had seen this same image before, but where?

The sketch that Cassidy drew from her last vision. That was it!

I would never be able to verbalize the peace that flooded my soul from seeing Mr. Jonas again, this time smiling and finally at rest.

It goes to show you that even in death, your reputation is known. I prayed that I would always have a good reputation.

With the living and the dead.

At the end of the day, and the end of life, that's all you were left with. A good name. Or a bad one.

I walked away from the cemetery and walked toward my wife and son with new purpose. New conviction. A new desire to continue my mission.

Our mission.

Gulf Coast Paranormal was back.

Epilogue—Macie

Sherman whined in the seat behind me. As usual, he refused to sit in the back and behave himself. I rubbed his furry white head and offered him a sour cream and onion potato chip. He sniffed it once and turned away disgusted. Unlike me, he wasn't a snacker when it came to food. Sherman preferred his smelly cans of Nibbles. He whined again and then sank down in the seat with a snort.

He didn't want to be here. That I gathered.

I continued to snack on my chips as I stared up at the empty building, the once-popular Leaf Academy. There were heavy chains on the front door, and the windows on the bottom floor were boarded up. I wasn't getting in there tonight. Still, I had to come. I had to see it again.

Yes, I'd snuck down here before just to see the place. I wadded up the chip bag before getting out of the car. My eyes went to the roof, to the place where I assumed my sister had been pushed by an evil entity. If I believed the story that the Gulf Coast Paranormal team told me.

I did believe them, right?

Was it possible for a ghost to kill a living person? What was the maelstrom, exactly? And why had it taken Jocelyn but no one else?

The questions came back to me again and again. I didn't want to feel this way. I didn't want to continue to return to these questions. She was my sister. Jocelyn had been the only family I had left, not including our hypochondriac mother. But now Jocelyn, the only good thing I had, the only good person I knew, was dead.

No matter how much I liked the team members, I needed answers. And the only way I would get my answers would be to investigate this place for myself.

Wait! Was that movement on the roof? I swear I saw a person up there. Maybe a security guard? I squinted up at the sun and moved closer to the building. "Hey! Excuse me!"

Boy, that would be great luck to have someone let me in, just to look around. But nobody reappeared. Maybe I'd imagined it. Suddenly, a blast of wind ripped through the parking lot. Piles of dead dried leaves swirled around me. It was so weird—like a dust devil had dropped down on top of me and had every intention of blowing me away.

Sherman began to bark furiously in the car. What was happening? I couldn't stay here and get whipped to death by dead leaves and trash. Covering my face with my hands as well as I could, I made my way back to the car. I slammed the door, and as soon as I did, the dust devil subsided.

I leaned back in the seat trying to catch my breath. What in the world? Sherman whined and pushed his cold nose against me. "It's okay, boy. It's okay." I glanced at myself in the mirror and noticed at least a dozen dead leaves in my hair. I began picking them out, but Sherman began to growl.

He never growled, not even when other dogs were around. Sherman was a pleasant dog. A kind dog. What on earth was he growling at? I turned around in the seat and immediately spotted the problem.

I saw a boy. Dressed in a white shirt, black knee pants and black shoes. He didn't move closer to me but stared and stared hard. It was impossible to see his features from this distance, but I was certain his eyes were solid black. And full of hate.

My hands were shaking as I turned the key. I had to get out of here. Sherman barked like a mad dog. "I know! I know! Give me a second, Sherm!"

I turned the key over again and again. Nothing happened. *Oh, God! What is going on here?*

I heard a voice coming from my back seat. I knew that voice.

Go, Macie! Go!

"Jocelyn?" I gasped as I froze.

Go!

Finally, the key turned over and I managed to speed out of the parking lot. My heart was beating like a wild rabbit's. I needed to flee. Fight or flight. I knew what that meant now, but there was no fight in me. Just flight.

"Jocelyn, help me!" I said as emotion overwhelmed me.

But I heard nothing else. Just Sherman's whining, which finally subsided once I made it home.

God! The Leaf Academy was no joke. Something terrible was there. And it was waiting for me. It knew I was coming, eventually.

No way would I ever go back alone. I would hold Midas to his promise. We would go back there one day. One day soon, I hoped. But I had a lot to do, a lot to prepare for. I knew that now. This would be a spiritual battle. Another level of warfare, not your typical paranormal investigation.

Yeah, I'd been terrified when I saw the boy, but I was over it now. Instead of fear, I felt anger. Deep and abiding anger. For now, that would be the fuel I needed to fight.

Fight for Jocelyn. Fight for me.

Sherman crept up beside me. He whined once and laid his head in my lap. His dark eyes studied me as if he knew what I was thinking and didn't approve. Not at all.

"I know you're worried, Sherman. I know, but I must do this for my sister. She deserves to be avenged."

Sherman snorted once and closed his eyes. I closed my eyes too. I slept and dreamed about Jocelyn. We were kids. Playing. Laughing. I loved jump rope. We were counting the jumps. She always won, but I was ahead this time.

Fifty-one, fifty-two...and then she was gone.

Jocelyn was gone forever. She'd never come back, no matter what I did.

I woke up with that thought, but it changed nothing. I was going to go back. I was going to do battle even if it cost me my life too. I picked up the phone and thought about calling Midas but changed my mind and hung up.

I wasn't ready for the Leaf Academy. Not yet. But I would be. I was going to learn everything I could about paranormal investigation. I was going to go to battle ready to win. And that would start with prayer. I wasn't good at praying, but now was the time to practice.

I got on my knees beside my couch and began to pray...

Author's Note from M.L. Bullock

This is officially the second book I've written with my husband and fellow writer, Kevin. Honestly, I never thought this day would come even though he often helps me with plotting and whatnot. In fact, Kevin is a notorious plot master. Whenever I get stuck on a book project, he's the guy I go to. He has great intuition about people. Sometimes after a session of brainstorming, riding in the car, talking about books, I look at him and think, "Who are you?"

Fans should thank Kevin for saving Ashland Stuart. He was on the chopping block (briefly) during the writing of the original Seven Sisters series. Thankfully, Kevin talked me down from that cliff.

But Gulf Coast Paranormal is a different animal. It does feature ghosts and the paranormal, but the characters have grown a lot. Changed a lot. Strangely enough, it was not difficult catching him up on Midas and his many cases. Honestly, Midas and Kevin are very much alike.

No, Kevin is not Greek or filthy rich, but he is a caring leader. Always has been. Seeing him write Midas' character so easily, really identifying with Gulf Coast Paranormal's leader, blessed my soul.

I hope you too can see all the heart he put into his work.

This story was unique. It was my first "investigation" in a cave system, and it was great that it was a local park. Or at least pretty local. If you get the chance to go to the Cathedral Caverns State Park in Alabama, do go check it out.

For my part, it was a joy to have Cassidy back. I love Sierra—I mean, she's kind of me—but Cassidy has a piece of my heart too. She's creative and kind. She loves her GCP family and is committed to keeping them safe with her talents and gifts.

It is exciting to see this crew continue to investigate the paranormal. I look forward to bringing you more stories featuring our beloved characters. If you enjoyed the story, please consider leaving me a kind review. You can email me and follow me on Facebook, too. I love hearing from my readers.

All my best,

M.L. Bullock

Made in the USA
Columbia, SC
18 March 2024

33010997R00087